EMERGENCY

Other titles in this series

EMERGENCY

STAYING ALIVE

LISA ROJANY

Hodder
Children's
Books

a division of Hodder Headline plc

First published in the USA in 1997 by HarperCollins*Publishers*

This edition published in Great Britain in 1997
by Hodder Children's Books

10 9 8 7 6 5 4 3 2 1

A Catalogue record for this title is available from the
British Library

ISBN 0 340 69805 5

Typeset by Avon Dataset Ltd, Bidford-on-Avon, Warks

Printed and bound in Great Britain by
Mackays of Chatham PLC, Chatham, Kent

Hodder Children's Books
A division of Hodder Headline PLC
338 Euston Road,
London NW1 3BH

'Holding on . . .'

Kyle saw Sara look up and he heard the knock at the same time. Dagger was outside the operating room. He must be letting them know that the blood products had arrived. Kyle knew that because he was not suited up, Dagger could not enter the sterile environment. A nurse nodded and went toward the door.

Kyle wondered what they were going to do about Carrie's broken leg, then realized that at the moment, a broken leg was the least of the patient's many medical problems. Carrie looked horrible. She was hanging on by threads of human skill, technological wizardry, and, Kyle imagined, somewhere in that deep unconscious state of hers, sheer will.

To my parents – Avi and Janis Rojany, and Mary Marks. And to Tanni Tytel, Peter Seymour, and Flora Marks – for mentoring me in a world where not enough women get guidence from those with wisdom.

* * *

Thanks also due to Alfredo Camacho, Karen Bradley Follette, Nicole Shoshani, Brigitt Minieri Dynes, Gary Klein, Lisa Kopelow, and Debra Mostow Zakarin, for all their love and help over the past year – literary and otherwise.

1

'Hey, Max! How's it going, you big slug?' Sara Greenberg said jokingly into the pay phone.

'Slug? Like I want to be stuck in this house even half a day more?' Max replied ruefully. Max Camacho had been stabbed in the arm a week earlier while on duty in the Emergency Room at County Medical Hospital where she and Sara were volunteers. The wound had been a superficial one, but the doctors had suggested – and her parents had loudly and strongly agreed – that she spend a week in bed anyway. Max had obeyed, but she was going bonkers! There was only so much studying she could do for the upcoming SAT – the Standard Achievement Test – to get into college. And with Christmas in only a few weeks, she still had all of her shopping to do. 'If I read one more detective novel, I am going to lose what is left of my mind!'

'Well, look at it this way: At least you get to take

the test tomorrow. It would be pretty awful if you had to postpone it,' Sara reminded her. Max's parents had promised that if Max stayed in bed for the week, then she could take the SAT that Saturday.

'Yeah. Say, you heard anything about Dagger yet tonight?' replied Max, trying to sound casual but failing.

'Max, I'm not even on duty yet!' said Sara. 'How would I have heard anything?' Max's stabbing was the result of Dagger's troubles with a gang called the Icers. Dagger Fredericks had tried to get in good with them a few months before, stealing an expensive camera. A judge had assigned him volunteer time at the hospital since it was his first offense and his record was otherwise clean. When the Icers later robbed and beat up his grandmother, Dagger had agreed to help the prosecutors go after the gang members. That was when the gang sent someone to get to Dagger – by attacking his girlfriend. Dagger and Max were no longer an official couple, but Max still cared a lot about him – and Sara knew it.

There was a pause at the end of the line. 'Oh, I guess I kind of lose track of time these days. When you're stuck in bed all the time, days and nights just seem to melt into each other.'

'Well, I promise to keep an eye out for him.'

'Thanks, girl. I owe you one.'

'Listen, I've got to go. My shift starts in a couple of minutes. I'll call you during break—'

'Please deposit twenty-five cents,' interrupted a computerized voice on the pay phone.

'Later, Max,' said Sara.

'Oh, man! Wait!' Max practically shouted.

Sara quickly dug around in her pockets for more change. She waited for the clink of the coins. 'What? What's wrong?' she cried.

'I almost forgot to tell you!' Max gasped.

'Tell me what?'

'My guidance counselor called me today. She got a call from *two* schools – San Diego and UCLA. They're both willing to delay the admissions deadlines until they get the scores from the SAT!'

'Really?' Sara was so excited for her friend that she could barely suppress a scream of joy. Max had decided to attend college much later than most of Sara's peers. If she got in, Max would be the first in all of her family to graduate high school, much less attend college. Max had been worried for ages that since she had decided to apply to college so late in the year and did not yet have all her test scores, she would have trouble getting in next year. 'So if you take this SAT and do well, then you get to go!'

'Theoretically,' Max agreed. 'What I'm going to do about money, I have no idea. I'm just going to have to wait and see . . .' Max's voice trailed off. Sara could just imagine how excited Max must be.

Sara was really proud of her friend. 'Congratulations!' she cried. 'Now let's hope I can improve *my* scores. Otherwise, I may be in trouble.' Somewhere on the west side of the city tomorrow, Max and Sara would both be taking that test, each with hope for the future and what it held.

'Oh, please, Sara,' Max said sarcastically. 'It's hard to improve on genius.'

'Yeah, right,' Sara snorted. 'I have to go now. I'll try to call you later.'

Sara raced over to her locker, and slipped the short-sleeved burgundy volunteer shirt over her T-shirt. She clipped on her ID tag and threw her hair up into a ponytail. Racing out of the locker room, she arrived at Ms Dominguez's office for their nightly briefing a mere three ticks before the clock's second hand hit 6:01.

'Well, welcome, Ms Greenberg!' Ms Dominguez said to Sara. 'Nice to see you made it.' The small smile was genuine but the irony of the tone was not lost on Sara. The volunteer coordinator was very strict about schedules and procedures. Slacking and tardiness were on the top of her pet-peeve list.

'Hi. Sorry,' Sara said, catching her breath. The two other volunteers on her shift nodded hello. Sara noticed that one of them, Kyle Cullen, looked kind of dressed up in new shoes and a freshly ironed button-down. If he weren't wearing the volunteer shirt, she would have sworn he was going out on a date. He smiled at her, but before she could smile back, Ms Dominguez's phone rang.

'Yes?' Ms Dominguez nodded and said, 'Right away.' When she hung up, she addressed the trio: 'With Max gone, you're going to be short-staffed, so make sure you keep on your toes and check with Nancy or Connie if you find yourself with nothing pressing to do.'

Dagger grunted. 'Right. Like that ever happens in the ER,' he said. Kyle and Sara grinned. But Dagger had a point. The Emergency Room at CMH was usually so jam-packed with activity that there was no time to breathe, much less sit around and shoot the breeze. And Ms Dominguez knew that. It was just her little way of warning them that it was already busy tonight.

The three volunteers left Ms Dominguez's office and made their way into the ER. Nancy Chang, the admitting nurse for the ER, greeted them as they walked in. 'Kyle, go down to the blood lab and put in an order for twelve liters of the blood type that's on

5

this sheet. Now!' Sara watched as Kyle rushed off with the paper clenched in his hand. There was a real sense of urgency in Nancy's usually calm voice.

'Dagger, I want you to prep Trauma One,' she went on. Evidently there was a big one coming in. Thoughts of tests and college flew out of Sara's mind. She couldn't wait to hear what it was.

'Sara, I need you to handle the phones. I'm expecting a call from Dr Tytel, the on-call cardiovascular surgeon. Dr Milikove, the general surgeon, has been paging her. They're going to need all the specialist help we've got.'

Sara immediately sat down at the empty chair next to the admitting desk. She kept her eye on the ten phone lines that were used solely for doctors responding to ER calls from other areas of the hospital. 'What's going on, Nancy?' Sara asked.

'We've got an MVA coming in from another county hospital thirty-five miles away. The patient is being airlifted because they don't have a trauma center there. We don't know much, but the patient is twenty-two years old, female—' The EMS computer modem screeched and Nancy turned and pressed a button so the speaker could be heard. Dr Milikove rushed over. A few doctors and residents surrounded the computer which tied into Emergency Medical Services – only this call was coming straight from the helicopter. Sara craned her neck to hear above the static as Nancy prepared to take notes about this motor vehicle accident patient.

'This is EMS Air Two-Twenty, do you read?'

Nancy pressed the speaker button. 'EMS Air Two-Twenty, this is CMH, Dr Milikove and team standing by. Go ahead.'

It was hard to hear over the static. 'We got a two-two female hit broadside by an eighteen-wheeler in an intersection. Her vitals are weak.' Sara knew that vital signs were pulse rate, respiratory rate, and cardiac rhythms. 'She's immobilized on a backboard and she's got a cervical collar on. There's a bad break in the left femur. Broke through the skin. It's splinted. We gave her oxygen and about a liter's worth of IV fluids to expand her blood volume. That was about an hour ago.'

'EMS Two-Twenty,' interrupted Dr Milikove, 'I need results of the chest X ray, CAT scan, and the angiogram, stat!' he said into the speaker. He was acting unreasonably impatient. Some doctors, Sara had learned, behaved like they were kings or queens and everyone else was a servant. 'Jesus! Is this guy a numskull or what?' he said angrily to Nancy. 'They're due here in less than ten minutes! I've got to know what I'm dealing with!'

'Sorry, doc,' came the reply from EMS Air Two-Twenty. Dr Milikove winced at the familiarity. He obviously did not like being treated without the utmost respect. He just shook his head and listened to the static-filled reply from the chopper. 'Patient's aorta is torn. Level of damage unknown. You'll get the results of the actual tests when we land.'

'They've had those results for an hour already! What's the delay? Unbelievable!' Dr Milikove pressed down on the button. 'EMS Two-Twenty, what is your ETA?'

'ETA seven minutes. EMS Air Two-Twenty out.'

The phone line lit up. Sara grabbed for the receiver. 'ER,' she stated simply.

'This is Dr Tytel. Dr Milikove paged me?'

'Hang on, Dr Tytel. He's right here.' Sara handed Dr Milikove the phone.

'Tina, we've got a torn aorta coming in by air. Yeah. I don't know.' Dr Milikove nodded his head. 'I hope you're not planning on starting any new cases tonight, because I need you. Good. The team is here. Trauma Room' – he looked at Nancy who put one finger up – 'One. Yeah. About a two percent chance. See if you can find Weizmann. Yeah. Great.' Dr Milikove hung up. 'Okay, she's due in six. Let's get suited up. It's going to be a long night. If anyone knows where to find Dr Weizmann, will you please tell him to get his lazy bum over here?'

Sara knew that Dr Weizmann was the anesthesiologist. He was on Dr Milikove's team. Dr Weizmann wasn't lazy at all, but his goatee and long hair worn in a ponytail gave him the look of a grungy college student instead of the topnotch doctor that he was.

At the admitting desk, Sara continued to listen and watch in fascination as the reports came over the EMS computer. She was surprised when Kyle returned from the blood lab. 'Are you done already?' she asked.

'Yeah, the other hospital called ahead so the blood was already waiting when I got there. I just dropped it off with Dagger in the Trauma Room,' he replied.

Sara nodded. Kyle looked flushed and excited. It was not the first time that Sara thought that he looked especially cute, his light hair all messy and his eyes bright. She used to wish she and Kyle were more than friends. But ever since she had met and fallen for Josh, a patient at the hospital, she was glad Kyle treated her more like a friend than a potential girlfriend.

Thinking of Josh Morrison made Sara sad. After being with her for only three weeks, Josh had moved to New York. He had been admitted to a clinic that was experimenting with new treatments for his condition – cystic fibrosis – which was chronic, and as yet, incurable. Sara knew it was the best thing for Josh, but she missed him, too.

Kyle interrupted her thoughts. 'Let's go wait on the pad,' he suggested in a whisper. 'Come on! It's really cool up there.' He slipped on a pair of gloves and motioned for her to follow.

Sara wasn't sure whether she should, but everything looked under control. No ambulances were yet in the bay. Even Dr Weizmann, the anesthesiologist on Dr Milikove's team, had managed to get his 'lazy bum' into the ER. All the doctors and surgical nurses on the team were suiting up and getting ready. Some of the ER staff were heading up to the helicopter landing pad already.

Sara asked Nancy if she and Kyle could go up to help on the helipad. Nancy nodded. 'Good idea,' she replied, which surprised Sara since it was going to get busy so soon. But then Nancy added, 'You have ten minutes, kids.'

Sara realized that Nancy was humoring them. Nancy was like that sometimes. A serious and completely efficient person, she often encouraged the volunteers to see new things and to always look on the bright side of the situation, no matter how bad the tragedy looked in the ER. Nancy knew the helipad was exciting to see, so she was giving them a moment's break.

Sara and Kyle made their way over to the elevator banks. In seconds, they were on their way up. On the roof of the hospital, the helicopter pad lay waiting for its next arrival.

2

The night was crisp and clear, but it was chilly on the roof. Overlooking downtown and situated up on a bit of an incline, County Medical Hospital afforded a beautiful view of the city's lights from this height. Below, the cars on the city freeways snaked along curving lines through downtown. Blackened mountains rose high to the north, dotted with occasional lights inside the homes nestled within the hills. Stadium lights lit up bright white in an oval shape just a few miles away from the hospital. Kyle felt special being up there, surrounded by medical personnel in this dramatic setting. He turned to Sara and was about to say something to her when a steady chop-chopping broke the silence of the whooshing wind.

Kyle followed Sara's pointed finger toward the light of the rapidly approaching helicopter. Within seconds it seemed as if the rhythmic copter's noise turned into a deafening roar. The force of the chopper's blades as it approached the landing pad caused a gale-force wind to whirl around the team huddled on the rooftop. Sara's shoulder-length brown hair started to whip around her face and Kyle bent his head against the dust swirls.

The chopper was down. When the rotary blades slowed enough to allow approach, the team descended on its opening doors. Sara and Kyle stayed out of the way as they watched the gurney being unlocked from its supports inside the chopper. The patient was slowly lifted out.

What Kyle saw surprised him. Somehow he was expecting an older person. But even though the sheet was pulled up to her neck, a huge cut slashed through her chin, and a tangle of tubes dangled from her face and arms, he could see that the patient looked really young. Sara had told him on the way up the stairs that the patient's aorta – which pumped blood from her heart to the rest of her body – was torn. Suddenly, the phrase *broken heart* changed meaning for Kyle. In this instance, it was literally true. It was a grave injury and from the tone of Dr Milikove's voice, in all likelihood fatal.

Kyle and Sara followed the paramedics and the trauma team to the waiting elevator. It was soon too packed for the volunteers to fit and they knew better than to push. They headed around the corner to the stairs and raced back down all twenty flights to the ER. They arrived just after the elevator – four minutes from the time they had first left the ER.

As the patient was wheeled to Trauma Room One, the paramedic explained to the trauma team that the patient had been sedated so that she would not regain consciousness and interfere with the barrage of tests they had performed at the other hospital.

Dr Milikove snatched the patient's file papers from the paramedic's hand and said under his breath, but loud enough for everyone in the room to hear, 'Next time, when you're talking to a licensed physician, it would behoove you to address him as *doctor* and not *doc.*'

Sara whispered, 'I'd hate to be on his bad side!'

Kyle smiled, but he would have never admitted to Sara that he wished he had Dr Milikove's power – it would be a rush to be able to get people to tremble in their shoes at your mere presence!

Dr Tytel, the cardiovascular surgeon, appeared and immediately got the scoop from Dr Milikove. The patient was already surrounded by nurses, residents, and X-ray technicians, as well as an EKG tech and a respiratory therapist. Dr Milikove and Dr Tytel monitored the patient and gave orders that set off a series of comments from the various CMH staff members.

'Check the IVs, please.'

'Let's pump in more fluids.'

'BP down to one hundred two over sixty-two. Pulse – one hundred thirty-eight. Doesn't look good.'

'Order up more blood. Stat!'

'Already here, sir,' Dagger piped in. He pushed over the cart loaded with the bags of blood ordered by Nancy from the lab just minutes before. Kyle had almost forgotten that Dagger was there.

'Keep her ventilated.'

'She's decompensating!'

Dr Weizmann, the anesthesiologist, immediately began evaluating the patient's medication and fluid status in order to prep her for surgery. He looked more tense than Kyle had ever seen him before. 'Let's go! Let's get her to the OR!'

Dr Milikove broke in. 'Hang on there, doctor. she's got multiple injuries, pulmonary contusion, trauma to the brain, a punctured lung, a compound fracture of the left femur, and who knows what else right now that we haven't yet detected. I don't want to focus on the aorta alone at the risk of overlooking other injuries. What if she's got a broken neck? She could be a quadriplegic. Let's just stay calm until we've had a chance to evaluate all the results.'

Kyle saw Dr Weizmann look up and nod, then get

to work again. In the pecking order, the general surgeon and the cardiovascular surgeon called the shots. Dr Weizmann had no power to overrule them, though he was required to make his concerns known to the rest of the team.

Kyle, Dagger, and Sara watched as the patient appeared to stabilize. It was then that Dr Milikove decided to move her to the ER's operating room.

'I'm going to talk to the patient's parents,' Dr Tytel said to Dr Milikove, who simply nodded. Kyle had heard that the girl's parents had been sent on their way to CMH with a police escort long before their daughter had been airlifted so they could be present when the actual surgery started. As the chief surgeon in the patient's case, it was Dr Tytel's duty to explain what was going on to the young woman's scared parents.

Kyle watched Dr Milikove lead the long line of staff down the hall. Dr Tytel pulled Dagger aside. 'Go to the blood lab and get some extra blood products. Tell them it's my airlifted aorta case – I forgot her last name.' Dagger left. 'You, come with me,' she said to Sara. 'We may need you in the OR.' Kyle felt a pang of regret, wishing that he had been chosen. Being in an operating room to help was totally cool. Sara was lucky. 'But first we're going to talk to the parents.'

Volunteers were allowed to observe during surgery if they were asked to be in there to help for some reason or if they had special permission from the head nurse on duty. But a doctor could veto that permission anytime.

Kyle followed Sara and Dr Tytel on their way past the admitting desk. They veered to the right, while Kyle moved a crash cart that had been left in the middle of the walkway. He overheard Dr Tytel speaking. While checking the contents of the cart to make sure it was properly stocked, Kyle crouched down so he could hear what she was saying. 'Hello, I'm Dr Tytel. I'm sorry you had to wait so long,' she said. Kyle could guess that the words about to come out of her mouth were not going to be reassuring. 'Although she's alive, I am sorry to say that it doesn't look very good.'

Kyle peeked over the top of the cart. Sara and Dr Tytel's backs were to him. The parents were seated on metal chairs, gripping each other's hands. He ducked again and listened.

'What are Carrie's chances?' the father asked abruptly.

'Fifty-fifty,' Dr Tytel said softly. 'At best.'

Kyle heard a sharp intake and then a low wail followed by deep sobs. He peered around the corner and caught a glimpse of Carrie's mother crying. The father was quiet, searching the doctor's face for signs of hope which he did not appear to find. Kyle stood up and pretended to fill up the cart. He couldn't wait for the day when he could do surgery. He wanted to be a life-saving surgeon who worked on complicated organs like brains or hearts. But he knew from Ms Dominguez that *this* was the hard part of the job – when patients became people with family and loved ones, and not just cases.

'She's already improved her odds by surviving the trip to the hospital,' he heard Dr Tytel say. 'We're going in now to repair the aorta, but—'

Kyle heard a heavy stride down the hall and looked up in time to see Dr Milikove march over. His huge eyebrows were knitted into a fierce frown. Nancy followed him. He interrupted Dr Tytel, speaking in a low whisper. Dr Tytel listened and then turned back to the parents. 'I'm afraid I don't have time to tell you any more, right this minute. We need to operate while her vital signs are stable. I'll be out here again as soon as I know anything. Have you signed all your release forms?'

'It's all been taken care of, doctor,' Nancy said.

Dr Milikove strode away, followed by Dr Tytel. Nancy turned and nearly crashed into Kyle. He belatedly aimed the cart toward the supply room.

'Kyle! Watch where you're going!' she admonished him.

'Sorry, Nancy,' he mumbled. 'I was just—'

'I know what you were doing. You were listening to them talk about that girl, Carrie, weren't you?'

Kyle looked at her in surprise.

'Could anybody really be *that* engrossed in a crash cart's supplies?'

'No,' he answered sheepishly. Was he always as see-through as he felt with Nancy and Ms Dominguez? So much for being cool.

'I know things are sort of slow at the moment—'

'Can I watch for a while from the observatory?' Kyle interrupted. 'If I promise to stay out of the way?'

Nancy finally agreed, but he was given only half an hour. 'And mind the loudspeaker,' she said. To Kyle, the translation was that if a volunteer call came over the loudspeaker, it was meant for him.

Kyle nodded gratefully and went to store the crash cart in the supply room.

Carrie was having open-heart surgery and he was dying to catch a glimpse of it. He headed to the observatory. The observatory was a room attached to the operating room. It had a wall with floor-to-ceiling, one-way viewing glass. Its floor was elevated so you could look over the table. You could flip on a switch and hear what was going on inside. If too many doctors weren't crowded over the patient's prone body, you might even be able to watch the surgery.

Kyle flipped on the switch and watched in silence as the bypass machine was hooked up. The circulating team began to administer the first of the series of blood products. He watched in fascination as the surgeons made an incision over eight inches long, opening up the left side of Carrie's chest. Kyle had to gulp and breathe evenly as he watched the skin being parted and clamped out of the way. Inside the chest cavity, Kyle could see the bright blood and white bone as well as parts and pieces he could not identify. Kyle's eyes kept going back to Carrie's face to see if she could feel any pain, but behind the oxygen mask, the young woman's face was blank.

Dr Tytel spoke through her face mask. 'The tear in the aorta is worse than we originally thought,' she announced, her hands busily working inside the young woman's open chest.

A murmur went through the room. Four medical students Kyle recognized from other Friday nights were practically blocking his view of the patient. Sara stood at the back of the operating room, silently watching and waiting to be called on. He could see her face struggling with the desire to look versus her aversion to seeing the opened chest cavity. Neither Sara nor anyone inside the room knew that Kyle was there watching. 'I'm going to clamp it off and repair the injured area by preparing a graft to bridge it,' Dr Tytel said.

'More blood!' called out a doctor.

Because of the clamping and unclamping, Carrie began to lose blood. Sara's face went white, her mouth a grim line of worry. Kyle looked away from her to Carrie. The tech operating the bypass machine pumped more blood into her.

Kyle saw Sara look up and he heard the knock at the same time. Dagger was outside the operating room. He must be letting them know that the blood products had arrived. Kyle knew that because he was not suited up, Dagger could not enter the sterile environment. A nurse nodded and went toward the door.

Kyle wondered what they were going to do about Carrie's broken leg, then realized that at the moment, a broken leg was the least of the patient's many medical problems. Carrie looked horrible. She was hanging on by threads of human skill, technological wizardry, and, Kyle imagined, somewhere in that deep un-conscious state of hers, sheer will.

3

Sara looked up for a moment as Dagger appeared through the window. Her attention immediately went back to the patient as she watched the tech struggle with the blood levels. Carrie continued to lose and gain, lose and gain – the blood tech did a delicate dance and manipulation. More than twenty liters had been used so far.

'Most older patients would not survive this,' Dr Tytel said to the medical student at her left as she continued to repair the aorta.

Dr Milikove's simultaneous repairing of the punctured lung and other injuries was just as pressing as the aorta. Time seemed to freeze during the delicate and complicated operation. Sara always felt disoriented when she left the room where a procedure was taking place. Even if it was in an ER cubicle, Sara got so absorbed during a medical procedure that she forgot everything else.

'Brain damage looks to be less severe than we first thought,' Dr Milikove said, examining the results of an MRI and the CAT scan.

'What about her leg?' asked a medical student.

'Left leg will stay in that splint for now,' Dr Tytel said. 'We can fix it later when her body is not under so much stress.'

Sara watched as Dr Tytel and Dr Milikove hovered over the body. Then Dr Weizmann and Dr Milikove suddenly seemed to be arguing. Dr Milikove was known to get into arguments during surgeries. Sara wondered how he could concentrate. The moment passed.

Sara then felt a touch at her elbow. 'You can go now,' said a quiet voice. It was one of the nurses.

'Thanks.' As the door closed behind her, she almost ran smack into Kyle.

'Hey!' he said enthusiastically. 'Did you see anything? Was it completely awesome?'

Before she could reply, she heard Dagger do so. 'Sometimes you make me want to puke,' Dagger said as they made their way back to the ER's admitting desk. 'You were in that observatory, weren't you?'

'Give him a break, Dagger,' Sara said wearily.

Dagger laughed. 'Why should I? We're all running around like chickens with our heads cut off and he's slacking in that observatory. He acts like he's a doctor already.'

'So? That's how people learn, Dagger. If you're interested in watching, then why don't you just ask Nancy?' Sara said, surprised to find herself sticking up for Kyle when she was just as often joking with the others about Kyle's weird intensity.

'I work just as hard as—' Kyle began.

'Oh, now you're *defending* him? Is something going on that I don't know about?' Dagger asked sarcastically.

Sara saw Kyle's head whip in her direction. Wasn't he going to say anything in her defense? 'Get over it, Dagger,' she said.

Just as Dagger was about to start an argument, the loudspeakers rang out, 'Volunteers to Admitting. Volunteers to Admitting.'

'Right here, Nancy!' Dagger said gallantly with a mock bow, as they came up to the admitting desk.

'Where have you guys been?' Nancy asked, ignoring him.

Sara looked around. In the last half an hour, seemingly out of nowhere, the ER had gotten packed. It was always like that. One minute calm, the next minute total chaos.

'I've got patients backing up and there's something weird going on here,' Nancy said. 'Must be a flu because I've got ten people complaining about severe stomach pains and all of them have a rash of some sort. Sara, you start getting patient information from them in the waiting room. Dagger, cubicle three has a teenager with a cut hand. He's pretty spaced out, so just keep an eye on the kid and his friend until we get a doctor in there. And Kyle, supplies in the cubicles are down again. Your turn.'

Kyle barely suppressed a groan and shuffled off toward the supply room to pick up a cart. Sara was glad it wasn't her. Restocking was the most boring and tedious of the jobs the volunteers had to do.

Nancy handed Sara a clipboard with a stack of mostly empty admitting forms, and Sara walked toward the patient waiting area. Nancy had been right. There were ten patients sitting in the waiting room bent over or clutching their stomachs. Some were moaning. Sara did a mental coin toss to decide who was first, and headed to the left.

The first person was a man, about twenty-five years old. His face looked greenish and pale. He was sweating and his arms were wrapped tightly around his stomach, even though he was trying to look casual.

'Hi, I'm Sara. I'm a volunteer here, and I need to get some information from you before we can treat you.' She looked at him to see if he understood her. A lot of the patients admitted to the ER came from different countries or simply did not speak English.

'It's about darn time!' he said impatiently.

Well, that solved that. English appeared to be his mother tongue. 'Your last name?'

'I already gave that at the desk. That woman over there!' He pointed in the vicinity of Nancy.

'Yes, sir, I am aware of that. But you didn't tell *me,* and I need to know so I can pick your chart out of this pile and get the process started,' she replied sweetly. No need to be nasty back. The poor guy probably just felt really sick. How could you blame him for acting impatient?

He seemed stumped. 'Okay. Sorry about that, I'm just not feeling too good.'

'We'll get to that in a minute, Mr . . . ?'

'Shane. Charles Shane.'

'Address?'

'57011 North La Crescenta.'

'Phone?'

'555–8701.'

'Insurance?'

He rattled off the name.

'So, what seems to be the problem? Can you describe what you are feeling and when it started?' she asked.

'I went out to dinner early. When I got home I

started to feel a little woozy. My stomach started to act up. Then I broke out in these little red bumps. About half an hour later I got the . . . I had to . . . you know!' he muttered into his shirt.

'I get it, sir. Were you having difficulty going to the bathroom?' she asked quietly.

'Gee!' he said, clutching his belly. 'You people sure ain't shy! I got the runs, okay?'

Sara nodded. 'I'm going to take your chart over to the admitting desk and we'll get you in to see a doctor as soon as possible.' The patient grunted. Sara took that for a thumbs-up signal.

She started the process with the second patient. The symptoms the woman described sounded quite similar to Mr Shane's. The third patient's symptoms were also the same. By the time Sara got to the fifth patient, she had an idea about what might be happening. When she was done with the tenth, she was pretty sure. She went back to Mr Shane, who was still sitting there, looking greener than ever.

'Mr Shane?' Sara asked.

'Huh?'

'Mr Shane, where did you have dinner tonight?'

'Uh, I went down to the taco joint over on Tenth and Columbus.'

'Do you know the name of it?'

27

'Pepe's. Pepe's Tacos.'

'What exactly did you order?'

'Uh, I had two beef tacos and some chips. And a watery soda. Can you believe them guys get away with watering down their soda?'

'No, that's a crime for sure. Thank you, Mr Shane,' Sara said, trying to keep a smile from creeping onto her face.

The second patient with stomach cramps had also eaten meat at the same restaurant. So had the other eight. Sara went back to the admitting desk. 'Nancy?' Nancy was busy juggling three calls and filling out umpteen papers all at once. 'Hmmm?'

'I think there's an epidemic of some kind of food poisoning. All ten of those people out there with stomach cramps went to the same restaurant. They all ate meat. And they all seem to have similar symptoms.'

Nancy looked up at Sara and put down the papers. 'Hang on.' She finished the call and hung up. 'I suspected something like that. I hope it's not the same place that was giving people hepatitis last week.' Over a dozen people had been diagnosed with hepatitis after eating at a popular restaurant last Friday. 'Did you write all the information on their charts?' Sara nodded. 'Good. This is what you need to do for me. Go over to Health Services and talk to Jean. Get her to call the

Department of Health and Social Services' emergency number. Give her the name and address of the restaurant and the names of the patients. They'll call over and send someone down to inspect the restaurant and close it up if necessary. They may send in some of the restaurant workers to be tested for hepatitis, and they might come by here and get statements from the patients. Nice work, Sara. If you're right about the meat, you might be saving someone's life.'

Sara smiled. She felt like a good detective. 'What do I tell the patients?'

'Right now, nothing. We'll get them in to see a doctor as soon as possible. If they start throwing up, that's when we might have some real problems. None of them have vomited, have they?'

'One woman said she did before she came. Why? Do they have to have their stomachs pumped?' Sara had heard of people having tubes put down their throats and the contents of their bellies literally vacuumed out.

'We'll see. I'll page Dr Shoshani, the gastro-enterologist on call. He'll know what to do. Meanwhile, see if you can get to the admitting papers on the others out there. We just got three new arrivals, all with broken bones. Tonight seems to be copycat night or something!' Nancy picked up the phone and handed Sara another sheaf of papers. Sara thought that admitting was pretty routine as far as volunteer duties went, but at least she could run through SAT vocabulary words in her mind while she jotted down the information. Despite the vote of confidence from Max on the phone earlier, the SAT tomorrow was worrying her a bit and she wanted to get in the right frame of mind.

Sara headed out of the patient waiting room and over to the Health Services. She told Jean what was going on and gave her the name of the restaurant and the list of patients admitted. Then she headed back into the waiting room. Just as she passed Mr Shane, he grabbed onto her shirt. 'Miss? I don't feel so—' And before she could move out of the way, he threw up all over her shoes.

Sara fought down two simultaneous urges: to throw up herself because the smell was awful, and to push Mr Shane back into his seat. But this was her job! *I am a volunteer,* she admonished herself. *Volunteers help patients. They do not get angry with them for not feeling well.* 'I'll go get you something for that,' she mumbled.

'Sorry, I—' And he did it again. He was heaving now.

That was when it happened. As Sara turned toward Nancy's desk to get some help, stomach cramp patient

30

number two leaned over and threw up on the floor. As if on cue, almost all of the other stomach cramp patients began to vomit. The noise of heaving and retching hiked up in a crescendo of misery.

Sara was both disgusted and alarmed. She whirled around and tried to run to Nancy's desk, but she slipped and fell, sliding across the room on the slippery, partially-digested-food-covered floor.

By this time, Sam, the security guard, was up on his feet, his mouth at his walkie-talkie, calling in other guards. The waiting room, packed to the gills with suffering people, was beginning to register panic. 'I need housekeeping down here right now with buckets and mops – see if Mrs Kopinsky is around. I also need some orderlies to move these sick people out of here. I don't know. Some kind of flu!'

Nancy came rushing into the room just as Sara managed to get a grip on the wall and pull herself up. The AN took one look at the line of people throwing up and headed straight to the supply closet. 'Sara! Follow me! Where is that Mrs Kopinsky when we need her, hmmm?' Nancy was trying to joke with Sara.

Sara, breathing through her mouth as she stumbled after Nancy, didn't reply. Mrs Kopinsky, the house-keeper on duty Friday nights in the ER, was famous

31

at CMH for cleaning up and throwing out everything that wasn't nailed down. A few weeks ago, she had even accidentally thrown away a patient's prosthetic leg! But right then, Sara couldn't find much humor in Mrs Kopinsky's convenient absence.

As Nancy loaded up a cart with buckets and towels, she ordered Sara to wipe herself down and to cover her clothes with a gown for the time being. 'You hand them each a plastic bag and then you take them into cubicles. Numbers thirteen through twenty are open. Double them up if you have to, but tell them what you are doing so they don't panic. Tell them to sit down and put their heads between their knees. If they have to vomit, ask them to please use the bags!'

Sara nodded, grabbed a handful of plastic bags, and headed into the waiting room. It was total chaos. The stomach cramp patients were all doubled over. There were kids screaming and adults yelling. Other patients had started to spill out into the hall. Sara headed to Mr Shane.

'Mr Shane! Take this. We're taking you into a room. Here!' She pulled him to his feet, shoved a bag into his hand, and led him over to cubicle thirteen. He sank into the chair gratefully. 'You're going to be fine, Mr Shane.' She helped him lean over into his open lap. 'Just relax. And if you can, try to aim into the bag if you need to throw up. All right?' Mr Shane gave her a miserable look and dropped his head between his open knees.

Sara did this ten separate times, glad for the small miracle that some of the stomach-cramp patients were related to one another and didn't mind being put in a small space with other people vomiting right next to them. By the time she was done, Dr Shoshani was already examining Mr Shane and a bunch of residents were examining the other patients. The waiting room had been restored to calm and the floor had been cleaned and disinfected. Even Sam was back at his desk, reading the paper and keeping a wary eye on the post-panic patients still left in the waiting room. Sara, though, was a complete mess.

Nancy caught up to her near the desk. 'Take these,' she said, handing Sara a pair of green surgical scrubs. 'I want you to go down into the women doctors' locker room. There are soap, shampoo, and towels right near the showers. You can't continue tonight looking' – here she paused and smiled – 'and smelling like that. Then take your break. You deserve it. I'll see you back here in a bit.'

Sara grinned ruefully. She was a little disgusted at herself as well.

'Oh, and don't forget to run those shoes under some

water.' Nancy wrinkled up her nose good-naturedly.

Sara looked down at her sneakers and sighed. If only she had covered them up with those plastic sheaths that they were told to wear just in case. But she had forgotten. Max was lucky she was not volunteering tonight. At that moment, Sara would have given anything to be in a nice, clean bed.

4

When Dagger parted the curtain to cubicle three, he just stood there in a sort of shock for a second. It wasn't the strung-out teenager who sat hunched in a chair against a corner with a hand wrapped up in a bloodied shirt that was so amazing. It was the girl. He could not believe his eyes. Right in front of his eyes was the most beautiful girl he had ever seen. She was leaning over the boy. His hand was bleeding and she was trying to keep him seated. He was super jumpy and his eyes were ringed in dark purple, and red as blood. Drugs, Dagger guessed.

'Hey,' Dagger said softly. 'I'm a volunteer. I was sent to see how you guys were doing.'

The girl whipped her head around in alarm then flashed a nervous smile at him. Dagger's heart practically stopped. She was hot! And didn't he know her from somewhere? He was about to turn on the charm when he suddenly felt guilty. It was Max. He was missing her big time. Volunteering on Friday nights just wasn't the same without her. Even if they were no longer together as a couple, he still liked knowing that he would see her. Now, he couldn't even go to visit her at home because her parents were on the rampage, convinced that her stabbing was his fault.

Thinking about Max cooped up at home in bed made him feel guilty again. If he hadn't been in trouble because of the Icers in the first place, Max never would have been hurt. She would be safe. He was glad that she was healed, but for the rest of his life, he would feel responsible for her injury – as well as Gran Tootie's. For the millionth time, he wondered what had possessed him to ever want to get involved with that gang.

Instead of trying to charm the girl, Dagger sat down in a chair. He smiled but kept his distance, so as not to scare either of them. 'What happened?' he addressed the girl.

The girl shot a look at the boy, who in turn shook his head fiercely. 'He . . . uh . . . ran into a wall,' she said lamely.

Dagger knew she was lying, but he figured he'd go along, since the kid looked like he might lunge out of the room, given the chance. He nodded at the hand. 'Can I have a look at that?'

'No!' the kid cried out. 'I'm fine. Me and . . . uh,

my sister, we was just on our way out of here. Huh, sis?'

The girl looked scared again, but she said to the boy in a low voice, 'No. We're going to stay here until the doctor comes and fixes your hand. Then we're going to leave. Isn't that right?' She looked at Dagger with wide eyes; she was telling him to agree with her.

'That's right,' Dagger replied, feeling somehow privileged that she took him into her confidence by assuming he would be on her side. 'The doc'll fix you up. Could you at least hold that hand up, elevated above your heart? It'll keep the bleeding down. Good. Now, what's your name?'

'I'm Kyra Mar—' But the boy elbowed her in the ribs before she could finish. He clearly didn't want her last name known. 'Kyra,' she repeated.

'Kyra, I'm Dagger. How come your brother won't let me see his hand?'

Kyra looked blank for a moment, then recovered herself. Dagger took this to mean that she and the boy were *not* related. They sure didn't look anything alike. The girl was tall and strong-looking, with long brown hair and dark chocolate-colored eyes. She was also washed and her clothes looked clean. Her 'brother' was dirty and looked like his clothes hadn't been washed in weeks. He was short and delicate, with a huge mop of sandy-colored hair and blue eyes.

'He's just worried that it's going to hurt too much,' Kyra finally replied.

'Well, you got him to the ER. That was the right thing to do. Looks like it's bleeding pretty badly.'

'Yeah, he was scared from all the blood and he fainted right after—' Kyra began, but again the boy elbowed her.

Dagger continued, 'And since you have to wait for a doctor anyway, why don't you let me at least give you a clean towel for that?'

Kyra plopped down on the hospital gurney and looked at the floor. The boy's eyes met Dagger's and then darted away. *I've seen that look before*, Dagger thought. *He looks scared and guilty. It's not just the drugs he's on. This kid's in trouble and he knows it. And so does this girl who dragged him in here.* Dagger decided to try a different tack. 'Don't we go to the same school?'

The boy snorted in disgust. Kyra looked at Dagger, who tried to appear as gentle as he could. 'Yeah, I'm a junior. I've seen you around,' she said in a voice barely above a whisper.

'Do you live nearby?' asked Dagger.

She nodded her head. 'Off Central, near Ninth.'

Cool. She was from his neighborhood.

Kyra glanced at the boy and immediately shut up. He was glaring vehemently at her.

Suddenly Dagger really wanted to find out what had happened. What kind of trouble were these kids in?

He moved closer to where Kyra stood and sat down on the gurney. 'Are you all right?' he asked softly.

Kyra's eyes met Dagger's and slowly filled with tears. She nodded.

'Are you worried about your friend?' Dagger indicated the boy.

Kyra nodded again.

'You know you're going to have to tell someone sometime what happened so we can fix it. The nurse said that you told her his thumb is practically cut off. If we wait too much longer, he could lose it,' Dagger said gravely.

Kyra's head dropped onto her chest. Dagger let his glance fall on the boy. He was silently staring at the girl, willing her to look up so he could tell her to shut up. But Kyra's head stayed down.

'Don't you want to help him?' Dagger asked.

Silence.

'It's only going to get worse. If you don't talk to us, you'll have to talk to the cops. They might not be as understanding,' Dagger explained. 'You don't have to tell me about him. Just you. Okay?'

A few moments later, Kyra spoke softly. 'I'm Kyra Martin. I was just dropping by. I didn't even know what was going on—'

The boy leaped to his feet and lunged at her. 'Be quiet! Don't say nothing! You—'

Dagger was on his feet in a split-second and pushed the boy back into the chair. 'Chill out, man! Do you want to get some help or not?' His heart was pounding as he loomed over the boy.

The kid's shoulders slumped in defeat. Dagger gave Kyra a nod. He could tell she was impressed with him. 'It's all right,' Dagger said, feeling really in control. He liked having this girl look up to him. 'Why don't you just start from the beginning, you know? It can't be that bad.'

'Yeah, it could,' said the boy sullenly. 'You got no idea.'

'Shoot,' said Dagger.

The boy eyed him suspiciously. 'Well, I was . . . uh, where do I start, man? I don't know where to start. This crap's been goin' on for so long, there ain't no *real* beginning.'

'Try me.'

'It's my mom. She's – well, she's trying to make ends meet – every month the same thing. She got home from work tonight and . . .' He looked at Dagger to gauge his reaction.

'Go on,' said Dagger.

'I live over in the projects by Union Station. Kyra, she brings me food and stuff, you know? We used to go to Ramsey together. She ain't got nothin' to do with nothin'. You get me, man?'

'I get you,' Dagger said, calming as the kid opened up.

'Well, my mom, she didn't pay the rent this month. I didn't know. And the landlord, he came over. Usually she can talk him out of it. But this time he started to beat her. And, uh – I don't know what came over me, but when I heard her screamin', I just lost it and' – he paused, getting choked up – 'and I think . . . I think . . . he's dead.' He started to sob.

Dagger had seen a lot on the streets. He'd seen people get killed and he'd seen people strung out on drugs, but somehow he wasn't prepared for this. He knew he had to proceed cautiously, because now with this information, the question of whether he had to bring the cops in was gone. It was a given. This was a confession. He spoke calmly. 'What's your name?'

'Johnny Vine.'

'How did you cut your hand, man?'

'A bottle. I used a wine bottle. It broke on the dude's

head and cut my thumb,' the boy stated simply.

'Okay, listen,' Dagger said. 'I'm going to get the doctor now. We're going to get your thumb taken care of best we can. Is your mom still at home?'

Johnny shrugged.

'Is the guy?'

'I guess.'

'Because they're going to want to talk to her,' Dagger explained. 'And you're going to have to talk to the cops.'

'But they're going to throw me in the joint!' he protested.

'You're underage and if you're telling the truth, it sounds like you were defending yourself and your mother.' Dagger looked up at Kyra for confirmation.

'I swear,' she said, nodding vehemently. 'What he says is all true. I was out in the hall the whole time.'

Dagger nodded and parted the curtain, slipping outside. He briefed Nancy on his conversation with the two kids and she quickly got on the phone. Dagger stepped back into the cubicle with the teenagers, who did not speak. They looked exhausted. He wondered how this kid could have kept going so long, losing as much blood as he had. Dagger suddenly felt very young himself – and helpless. Why did life have to be so hard for some people?

Nancy appeared about ten minutes later with two

cops and a doctor. Dagger stayed and watched as Johnny allowed the doctor to unwrap his hand and throw away the bloody shirt. The thumb was indeed severed quite badly from the palm. The doctor pulled over a cart and told Johnny he was going to inject him with something that would numb the area so he could try to stitch it up. He then began to clean the wound. Once Dagger saw the boy was okay, he parted the curtain to where the cops stood.

He told them what he had learned while they took notes. One of the cops went to a phone to call in the location of the body, then they both went inside to wait for the teenagers.

Kyra came out a moment later. 'Could you show me where the restroom is?'

'It's on my way,' Dagger said, smiling at Kyra. He admired her sideways as they walked slowly down the line of cubicles. Then he noticed a cleaning crew coming from the waiting room and wondered what he had missed.

At that moment Kyra tripped. Dagger reached out to save her from the fall. He grabbed her right before she would have crashed into a cart.

'Are you okay?' he asked.

'Just tired, I guess,' she explained, watching Dagger closely.

'Well, please allow me to escort you safely to your destination,' he said gallantly, tightening his arm around hers. She smiled at him, and he grinned as they rounded the corner.

Dagger looked away just in time to see Sara walking toward them carrying a pair of surgical greens. He felt the smile melt off his face. He knew that the first thing Sara would do was run and call Max about this.

Sara's eyes narrowed when she saw the girl holding on to his arm, but then she just smiled smugly and passed them with a cheerful, 'Hi, Dagger!'

Dagger winced.

Kyra coughed delicately into her hand. 'What was that *smell*?'

Dagger groaned. 'I'm not exactly sure. Here we are,' he said as they arrived at the women's bathroom. 'I'll wait outside for you.'

While he waited, Dagger got to wondering. Why did he feel that twinge of guilt earlier? Max had broken it off with *him*! And Kyra was really cute. Why not ask her out?

5

Sara scrubbed her face with liquid soap again, trying to get the stench of vomit out of her nose. She thought about her mother. Should she call her? She had been so angry when her mom had tried to contact her again after all this time. She had sent a few letters in the past, but Sara had always thrown them away unread, and eventually they had stopped coming. Until a few weeks ago. Sara had received another letter, and this time she had chosen to open it. She had decided not to think about it for a little while, but then had become so angry that she wrote back a biting reply. There was no way she could have responded positively. So what if her mom had stopped drinking? She had beaten Sara so many times that Sara used to flinch whenever she walked by her. But now Sara felt more in control, and she found herself reconsidering.

Sara stepped out of the shower and dried herself off. She wrung out the clothes that she had been wearing and pushed them into a plastic bag. Shivering, she slipped into the surgical greens and tugged on her sopping wet sneakers. She passed the pay phone and considered calling Max, but a quick check of her watch told her that she'd been gone twenty minutes already. She rushed to the locker room and dumped her sopping clothes bag inside the locker. Then she made her way back to the ER's admitting desk.

Sara was about to tell Nancy that she was going to the cafeteria when she caught sight of Dagger now helping with the new patients in Admitting. He looked totally absorbed. Kyle rolled by her with the supply cart piled high. An hour later and he was still at it, poor guy!

Directly in front of Nancy's desk a guy stood behind an elderly woman holding a Jack Russell terrier on her arm. Nancy was trying to explain to the woman that they didn't treat animals in the ER, but the woman was not listening. 'He's smart, my Jocko is,' she insisted. 'He's smarter than my son, if you ask me.'

'Ma'am, this is a busy ER. We do not treat animals here. You have to go to a vet for that,' Nancy said patiently.

'Honey, the vet is closed,' the woman replied confidently. 'It's Friday night, you know. Besides, like I said, there's something wrong with his paw. It's all red.'

'I understand that, ma'am, but we still don't treat animals here. How about this? I'll give you a phone book, and you can look up the name of a twenty-four-hour veterinarian.'

'It's highway robbery what those twenty-four-hour guys charge! No, I want Jocko to get the best treatment. No dog doctor for him. He's a smart boy. He knows the difference.'

Sara smiled. The old lady was holding her own. Sara marveled that amidst all this craziness Nancy didn't ever lose her temper.

'Ma'am, why don't you sit down, and I'll have someone bring you a cup of coffee. I need to get to this next patient.' Nancy nodded to Sara, inclining her head toward the kitchen. It was clear to Sara that the woman was crazy and that Nancy was just trying to be nice to her until she had to kick her out.

Grumbling, the elderly woman mumbled to her dog, ' . . . think they're going to send you to some quack. Harumph! We'll get you some nice coffee and . . . Hey!'

Nancy looked up, eyebrows raised.

'Got any doughnuts? A bagel?'

'We'll see, ma'am.'

Sara felt sorry for the woman, who was obviously out of her mind, and was about to go fetch the refreshments when she noticed that the man who had been waiting patiently was holding his two hands in front of his belly. The strange thing was that his hands appeared to be wrapped around something. Sara looked closer. That was when she realized that he was holding a metal spike – and it was coming straight out from the middle of his gut! She stopped in her tracks, her hand to her mouth. Where was all the blood? She didn't get it. Why wasn't he bleeding?

Sara ran to get the elderly woman some coffee and a cookie for her dog. She almost spilled it all in her haste to return to the desk. Nancy had already called in another surgeon since Dr Milikove was with Carrie dealing with some post-operative complications. Sara overheard Nancy trying to keep the man calm by chatting with him quietly. 'And how did you manage to get here?'

'Well, after I realized what happened, I slid off the roof holding on to the spike. I didn't know why it wasn't bleeding. But I knew I had to get over here. No one else was home, and I was afraid to get in the car in case I pushed it through my back, so I just walked over here,' the man explained.

'You *walked*?' Nancy asked. Even she was astonished.

'Yeah. Real slow,' he replied.

Sara could not believe it. The guy was smiling! He

had a stake through his belly and he was still in a good mood!

Dr Kadin, the surgeon, arrived and introduced himself to the patient. 'So, looks like you've gotten a little overdose of iron, hmmm?'

The patient smiled and tried to reach out his hand to shake the doctor's.

'No! No, please, don't move!' Dr Kadin said. 'I just want to look at you a little closer before I decide where we're going to take you. The only reason you haven't bled all over the place is because you were smart and you didn't move it.' He lifted the man's shirt to get a look at the stake. 'Was this a new piece of equipment?'

'I already thought of that, doctor,' the man replied. 'It's old, and there is rust on it. I bought all the iron stakes secondhand. Wanted to save a little money and do the work around the house by myself. Hard to find a good contractor these days . . .' His voice trailed off as he looked down at the black rod coming out of his belly. The man then reached into his shirt pocket. He pulled out a huge ring of keys. 'These are starting to pull on my collar. Aches a bit. Would you please—?'

Just then something furry whizzed by and jumped in front of Sara's face. It was growling. It leaped up again and yanked the keys out of the man's hand, in the process crashing into the stake and pushing it downward. The man yelled out in pain, grabbing the stake.

'What the—?' cried the doctor, lunging forward to keep the man from pitching forward onto the ground. But Jocko was in the way and the doctor stepped on the dog's tail. The dog yelped loudly.

'Jocko!' screamed the old lady.

Dr Kadin was too late. The man fell to the ground. The stake pushed through and was sticking out of the man's back at a ninety-degree angle. Blood started to flow out onto the floor as if a finger had been pulled out of a dike.

'Jocko! You bad boy! Are you all right? Those are *not* mommy's keys!' the crazy pet owner admonished. 'I don't see so well. I trained him to get my—'

'Dagger!' Nancy called. 'Help Dr Kadin. We need to get this patient—'

Dr Kadin was already surrounded by hospital personnel. A resident and a nurse were hoisting the man onto a gurney. They laid him on his side.

'Into the Trauma Room – stat!' ordered Dr Kadin. 'Nancy, get a hold of Dr Weizmann. I'm going in.'

'Dr Weizmann is still in post-op with Dr Milikove. How about Dr Peoples?' Nancy offered.

'Fine.'

'Trauma Room Two okay?'

'Yeah. Is it prepped?'

'Yes, doctor.'

Sara whirled out of the way as Dr Kadin wheeled the man into the Trauma Room with Dagger and other personnel alongside. The patient was already out cold. Sara marveled at how he had lasted so long without passing out. Now it was in the doctors' hands to save him.

No one seemed to need Sara at the moment, and she was still up for a quick break. She told Nancy she was going to the cafeteria. Nancy nodded absent-mindedly and Sara left. Squishing down the hall in her wet sneakers, she felt conspicuous and ridiculous. Halfway there, she changed her mind and decided to head into the locker room. She had cookies in there. She could take them into the cafeteria and get a soda. Moving her wet bag out of the way, she fiddled around in her backpack until she found the cookies.

Inside the cafeteria, she was surprised to see Kyle seated in a corner, chugging down a soda. She got a soda and sat next to him. He wrinkled his nose.

'Don't you dare, Kyle Cullen,' she warned, feeling grumpy and dirty despite the shower and her clean hair. No matter what she did, she couldn't get that smell away from her.

Kyle opened his eyes wide at the tone of her voice. 'Well, excuuuuse me!' he said. 'At least you *look* great. It's just that—'

'Can it, Kyle. I—' Sara was about to make a snotty retort when she realized that there was simply nothing she could do about it. Her hair stank. Her feet stank. She stank. And that was just that. 'You're right. Can we change the subject?'

'Sure,' Kyle replied. 'So how's Josh?'

Sara eyed him warily. Why was he asking about Josh all of a sudden?

He seemed to recognize that the question was a bit unexpected. 'I was just wondering. I mean, I know that you two got close.'

Sara fiddled with her straw. 'Yeah, well, he's doing all right. I mean, he's still getting that new treatment in New York. It's not like a cure or anything. It's just to help with the symptoms, the chronic respiratory problems and stuff. He sounds great.'

'Do you talk every day?' Kyle asked, crushing his can, tossing it toward a recycling container – and missing by a mile. He smiled sheepishly and got up to put the can where it belonged. 'Sorry. Where were you?'

'We try to talk every day. It's just really strange knowing that I won't see him again for a long time.

It's starting to feel a little like a dream. Especially being back at the hospital again and not having him to visit upstairs. It's weird,' she admitted. She wasn't sure why she was being so honest with Kyle. Maybe it was because even though he was annoying sometimes, he was a pretty good listener. 'Hey, what's going on with your brother?' she asked. 'How's he feeling? Any better?'

Kyle looked down at his fingers splayed on the table. 'Well, he's been in that place for about a week. At first they thought he would just go for a few hours during the day, but they say he's suffering from depression – like *real* depression.'

Sara nodded sympathetically. That whole ordeal must be hard for Kyle. When his brother had gotten in that car accident a few months ago, one of his best friends had died and another had lost his feet when a guard rail had sliced through the car. Alec was being held responsible since he had been driving drunk. There was still a very real possibility that he might spend time in jail.

'Not only that – he's having thoughts of suicide. My parents are pretty shaken up. This is one thing we never even thought would happen.'

'He didn't try to, did he?' Sara said, leaning into the table feeling shocked. She knew what it felt like to get that depressed. It was pretty awful.

'No. But last week I found a will that he wrote up on the computer. It was totally pathetic.Like he willed my dad all his sports trophies, and he willed me all his picture albums so that I would tell my kids about him one day. When I printed it out and showed my parents, they nearly lost it. Next thing I know, Alec is calling me a traitor and he's stuck in a hospital for depressed people.'

Sara was silent. Man! Kyle must feel like it was totally his fault! 'You know, Kyle, you did the right thing!'

Kyle would not look up at her. She saw his hand tremble and her heart suddenly went out to him. She wanted to comfort him. But how did she do that with a guy she knew kind of liked her – without giving him the wrong idea? She didn't know, so she just sat there. 'You might have saved his life!' she said. And as she said it she saw a tear drop onto Kyle's hand.

Oh, no, she thought, *don't let him cry. I don't know if I can take this!* She wanted desperately to change the subject, but she knew that was rude and insensitive.

Kyle was silent. Then he looked up at her, his eyes bright and glassy. 'I am really worried about him. What if he does something stupid? I mean, it would kill my parents. Alec is their favorite, you know?' His voice broke. He slipped away from the table and Sara watched him go get another soda. By the time he made it back to the table he had gotten a grip.

'We'd better get back,' she said.

'We still have five minutes. Want to go by post-op and find out what happened to that girl, Carrie?'

Sara smiled. It was so like Kyle to get totally into the nitty-gritty of these operations. Sara preferred the people side of medicine so far, while Kyle showed a definite propensity for the bloody side. 'Sure,' she replied. 'But we better make it quick.'

6

'Where were you guys?' Nancy asked as soon as she laid eyes on the two volunteers. 'Sara, I know I sent you on break, but Kyle, you're ten minutes late from yours!'

Kyle knew that by checking up on Carrie he had extended his break much longer than he should have. And he knew Nancy knew it. No use lying about it. 'I lost track of time,' he admitted.

Nancy searched his face. 'Kyle, you know better than that. Next time, carry a watch. There are rules here for a reason. I need volunteers here at all times. And we're short-staffed without Max. I'm sorry, but I'm going to have to mention this to Chelly Dominguez.'

It was the first time that Nancy had ever issued a warning that was more of a threat than a gentle reminder. Ms Dominguez was tough on her volunteers and did not put up with any messing around.

Volunteering was too important to Kyle for him to get in trouble with the coordinator.

'Listen, Nancy. I'm sorry,' Kyle said, the apology somewhat mumbled. He hated looking like a bad child in front of Sara – in front of anyone, for that matter. Sara was nice enough to pretend to be watching Dagger over in the admitting area. *Damn!* Ms Dominguez would eat him alive when she found out! He was screwed.

The doors to the ER suddenly slammed open. Two paramedics rushed in from the ambulance bay with a man on a stretcher. The sheet over his body was splotched with blood.

Though she had been talking to them only a moment before, Nancy obviously had been waiting for this. The subject of Kyle's rule-breaking was closed for now. 'Trauma Two, guys,' she said. 'The neurosurgeon's on his way down.'

A pack of residents surrounded the patient as they wheeled him to the crash room. He was about twenty years old, and he had been shot. This was not the first gunshot victim Kyle had seen in the ER. At CMH, a county hospital situated smack in the middle of an area known for its gang activity and drug wars, shootings were commonplace, especially on the weekends, and Fridays were always busy nights at the ER.

At Nancy's urging, Kyle and Sara followed the stretcher in case someone was needed to run to the blood lab or to fetch a piece of missing equipment. A pack of surgical interns were on their heels. Since CMH was also a teaching hospital, the interns and residents were often present in the ER and the doctors in charge would quiz them and ask them to make preliminary diagnoses so they could learn how it was all done.

The paramedic was filling in the neurosurgeon, Dr Zakarin, as he checked the chart. 'Two-zero Hispanic. Caught in the middle of crossfire approximately twenty minutes ago. One bullet grazed the skull near the left temple, the other entered through the back of the neck. Penetrated spinal cord. Caliber of bullet unknown – but it was big enough to hurt.'

Dr Zakarin's mouth twitched and he frowned. Jokes of this kind were often made in the ER, but it was generally acknowledged that they were not said aloud if the patient could hear.

The paramedic continued, 'We gave him CPR and put him on a ventilator. We don't know exactly how long he wasn't breathing before we got there. He can't move his arms or legs. He's heavily drugged but somewhat conscious.' Kyle wondered if the guy was so badly damaged that he would not make it. 'His name, according to the person who brought him in, is Benicio.'

Dr Zakarin looked right at Kyle. 'Get over to the blood lab and get me two liters of O-positive blood – stat!' He thrust a sheet of paper at Kyle.

Kyle grabbed the paper and raced off, leaving Sara behind to watch. She'd fill him in upon his return. At the blood lab he handed over the paper and waited for them to give him the bags. He fiddled impatiently with the rubbery gloves on his hands. The minutes ticked by. Finally, a woman returned with the blood and had him sign off, indicating what he had received and when. Blood supplies often ran low and the precious liquid was tracked more carefully than almost any other supply at the hospital. Everyone from volunteers to doctors was asked to give blood every few months to replenish the supply.

By the time Kyle made it back with the blood, a nurse was already standing at the left side of the stretcher, adjusting the monitors that tracked Benicio's heartbeat and respiration rate. An X-ray technician was at the far side of the room, fitting a newly developed picture of the patient's skull into a manila-covered sleeve and placing it next to his chart on a scratched steel table. There was a brown paper bag on the floor with the clothes the patient had been wearing before the shooting. They were shredded where they had been cut from his body by the ER staff.

A hospital-issue sheet was tucked around the patient from the rib cage down, but Kyle noticed many brightly colored tattoos plainly visible against his pale brown skin. A snake crept up his left arm, a naked woman slithered down his right arm, and a pack of wolves covered his nearly hairless chest.

Dr Zakarin leaned over the stretcher so that Benicio did not have to turn his face to see. 'Patient's eyes are open. He looks responsive and alert.' Kyle wondered why the lack of oxygen to the man's body before they gave him CPR didn't make him a vegetable.

Dr Zakarin reached over for the X-ray envelope and pulled out the films. He inhaled sharply, then addressed one of the surgical interns. 'Tell me' – he searched for the name tag on the nearest intern – 'Dr Mostow, what does the devastation caused by a bullet to the spine depend on?'

The intern began to recite from memory. 'It depends largely on where it enters the spine. The lower the bullet, the less the damage because the severed nerves will most likely be below the point of injury. Therefore, a shot to the lower back will likely paralyze the hips and legs, the arms will be okay. A shot to the vertebrae in the back of the rib cage will take the feeling out of the chest area as well. A bullet in the cervical vertebrae in the neck can paralyze everything from the neck down.'

'Good. And what do these show . . . Dr Jason?' Dr Zakarin held the X-ray sheets against a lighted box.

Another intern examined the sheets. 'These show a bullet lodged much higher than I've ever seen before. It has entered the area of the C-3 vertebral segment, near the base of the neck, and traveled upward through the spinal column, where it is plainly visible above the C-1 vertebra, the very first of the cervical vertebrae in the neck.' The intern shook his head and whispered to the intern at his side, 'It's in the back of the brain. I can't believe he's still alive. He should be dead.'

Sara must have overheard him because Kyle saw her mouth set in a straight line and her face go tense. She always seemed to take the patients' injuries to heart, as if she could *feel* their pain. Kyle didn't feel like that. Kyle had had a hard time with all the blood when he first started volunteering – no matter how much he wanted to forget fainting on his second night in the ER, Dagger wouldn't let him. But he had since come to feel more removed from the patients. They were more like subjects of study to him than they were to Sara. To Sara, they were just bundles of feelings.

For the next fifteen minutes, Dr Zakarin conducted a physical exam. Leaning over the stretcher, he asked, 'Can you hear me?'

The patient did not move. Dr Zakarin looked up at the ER nurse. Like many of the nurses in the ER, he spoke Spanish. 'If you can hear me, blink your eyes twice,' he said, translating for Dr Zakarin.

'Two blinks, rather than one, are less likely to be a reflex or an accident,' Sara whispered to Kyle.

Kyle was impressed. It was usually he who was full of all the medical information.

The blinks were weak, but they came one after the other.

'Follows commands with eye opening and closure,' Dr Zakarin said aloud for the benefit of the interns as he jotted notes on the chart.

He had the nurse-interpreter tell Benicio that he was going to ask him some questions and give him four choices as to answers. The patient was to blink twice at the answer he thought was correct. Dr Zakarin asked him the month, where he was, and what his name was, giving him various choices for each. Benicio answered all the questions correctly with the slow double-blink. 'Oriented as to time, place, and person,' Dr Zakarin said.

Taking a pen light, Dr Zakarin then shined a narrow

beam into Benicio's eyes. Each pupil constricted quickly. 'What does this reaction show, Dr Mostow?'

'If there was swelling in the brain it would have probably blocked the nerve that controls pupillary response. The patient's fast response time, coupled with his apparent alertness, might indicate that this is a spinal injury only and not one of the brain.'

Kyle whispered to Sara, 'I think that means that he'll be able to understand what's happened to him.' Sara nodded slowly, her eyes fixated on the patient.

Dr Zakarin then addressed Benicio again. 'Can you move your left leg?' The nurse-translator repeated it in Spanish. There was no response.

'Your left leg?' Nothing. 'Left arm?' Nothing. 'Are you trying to move your arm right now?' Two blinks but no movement. 'Now your right arm.' Again, nothing. 'Shrug your shoulders like this.' The nurse's shoulders went up and down, but Benicio's stayed put.

Kyle realized he was holding his breath. He wanted the patient to move!

'Turn your head to your right, toward me.' The head on the pillow moved slightly. 'Good. Now turn the other way.' The head moved slightly again. Kyle exhaled. 'Can you wiggle your nose? Good, good.'

Kyle caught Sara glancing at her watch. She moved closer to him. 'It's nearly midnight. I have the SAT tomorrow. I have to go.'

Kyle looked back at the patient. He wanted to wait to find out what the diagnosis was, but he also wanted to go home. He was tired. 'I'll go with you.'

They walked down to the locker rooms. Dagger ambled into the hallway just as they rounded the corner. 'Man! Seems like I haven't seen you guys all night long! Heard you're in trouble with Nancy,' he said to Kyle.

'Took too long on break.' Kyle scowled.

'Yeah? Well, listen to this. I worked in Admitting for almost two hours and not one of the patients spoke English! You think you had a tough night!'

Sara laughed. 'You guys meet me back out here and we can get escorts to go out to the parking lot – and the bus station,' she added.

Kyle knew she added that because Dagger took the bus. He did not have a car like Kyle and Sara did. Dagger lived only a few blocks from the hospital anyway. Pretty near Max's house from what Sara had said, even though Max and Dagger went to different high schools.

'No problem. We'll wait for you,' Kyle answered, following Dagger into the bathroom. 'So, who was that girl I saw you with earlier tonight?' he called out to Dagger.

Dagger went to the sink to wash his hands. 'Just someone I met. I asked her out on a date, that's all.'

'She was hot, man!' said Kyle. Dagger didn't reply. After changing their shirts, they went out into the hall where Sara was waiting for them. The three walked to the hospital exit to pick up their escorts, then went out to the parking lot.

'See you next week!' Sara said.

Dagger was almost around the corner when he called out, 'Sara! Tell Max good luck on her test!'

Kyle caught Sara's surprise. Did she know about that new girl? He couldn't tell. But if she did, he was sure that Max would soon. The escort walked them out to their cars. Kyle watched Sara drive away. *She may be emotional,* he thought, *but she sure is cute.* On his way to his own car, he thought about what might happen next week with Ms Dominguez. He was going to have to face the music, of that he was certain.

7

The alarm sounded in Max's ears and her arm automatically went out to pound the off switch. Then she remembered: *Today is the SAT.* She inched up in bed and rubbed her eyes. She had two hours to get ready, eat a good breakfast, and make her way down to the testing center for the test which would begin at eight o'clock. Although her arm didn't hurt her much anymore, she had not slept well. She was worried about the test.

She rolled out of bed with a groan. Never a morning person, Max was used to feeling like a slug for the first few hours of every day. If it was up to her, morning would not begin until ten. A shower would help.

'*Hola, mija,*' her mother said to her when she made her way downstairs.

'Hi, Ma,' Max replied, wishing, not for the first time, that her mother would keep some of that morning chipperness to herself. Max and her father were the same: Both treated early morning sunshine like a bad cold.

'I made you eggs, toast with jelly, and fresh orange juice. You eat it all so you will have energy for your test!'

Max poured herself a cup of coffee – something she rarely did. She was really feeling slow. She looked at the time: seven o'clock. She had fifteen minutes before she should hit the road. 'I should be done by noon,' she told her mom, finishing off the coffee and chugging down two glasses of orange juice. 'I'll drop Papa off at the shop and bring the car back to him when I'm done. Then I'll walk home.'

Her father entered the room, nodded to the women in his family, and sat down. He sipped on the black coffee his wife served him and perused the local newspaper. Neither of Max's parents had graduated from high school, but they both read the paper every day. And although they had no idea how to help their daughter apply to colleges, they were proud that she was considering it. If she got in, Max would be the first one in her family to go.

'*Lista?*' Max's father asked. 'Are you ready?'

Max nodded and gathered up her backpack, being careful of her bandaged arm. She kissed her mother good-bye and followed her father out to the car. After dropping him off at the little neighborhood electronics repair shop he owned, she slipped onto the freeway and made her way to the west side.

The community college parking lot was nearly full when Max pulled in. She had to drive to the far edge of the lot to find a space big enough to park the huge old sedan in. By the time she made her way through the deserted campus to find the testing auditorium, it was nearly eight o'clock. Where was Sara? They had agreed to meet in the room so they could sit near each other. Max didn't have time to look for her since the proctor was already handing out answer sheets.

Max plopped down in the closest empty chair to the front of the room. When she walked in, all she had absorbed was that the auditorium was packed with teenagers and a few adults, all sitting one seat apart to discourage cheating. A pencil and scratch paper were already at her place. Big clocks were placed on all four walls so the students could keep track of time. Test proctors who monitored the test-takers were wandering around asking people to place their belongings underneath their seats.

Max's heart was already racing from running to the testing site. Once she got her pencils out, she closed her eyes and tried to calm down. *Plop!* A wadded piece of paper hit her in the back of the head. She whirled around. There was Sara, four rows back, grinning wildly and giving her a thumbs up. Max smiled nervously and turned around again.

'Please, people, settle down!' the proctor said. 'Those of you who are here for the SAT are in the right room. If you're supposed to be taking individual achievement tests, you belong in the next auditorium down the hall.'

Max heard the shuffles and curses of the unlucky few who had gotten their room numbers mixed up. The proctor stood aside as they exited in a hurry. Then the proctor continued reciting the directions for taking the test.

Max tried to stop her heart from pounding as she filled in her answer sheet. She had heard that you got two hundred points just for filling in your name correctly, but she didn't know if that was really true. She was so nervous. *Chill, girl,* she told herself. *You've studied like a maniac for weeks. You're smart. Just pretend this is just another stupid pop quiz at school. No big deal.*

'Now, please open your booklets. Make sure you're on section one. We'll let you know when your time is up. Good luck!'

Max opened up the first section. It was a verbal section. Once Max got through the first few questions with ease, she felt a little better. The room was quiet as a graveyard.

Just as she finished the section, the proctor called time and instructed everyone to lay down their pencils. There were a few groans. Max turned around to look at Sara. Sara was inhaling and exhaling with her fingers in her ears to block out the noise. She had told Max that this was how she relaxed when she was nervous about a test. Some sort of weird meditation ritual. Even though it looked pretty queer, Max half-wished she had learned it because she was still pretty worked up.

The next two hours went like clockwork. The math sections were pretty easy and the English sections were fun, in a brutal sort of way. Max had one section to go when she realized that she desperately had to go to the bathroom. There was no way she could wait. She had two minutes before the next section began. She'd try to make a run for it. She raised her hand and the proctor excused her.

'But we won't hold up the test if you don't get back in time,' the proctor warned. Max winced, hating herself for forgetting the very first cardinal rule of test-taking: Always go to the bathroom beforehand. Another proctor would escort her to the ladies' room to make sure she didn't bring cheating materials with her.

As Max exited the room she noticed someone behind her. She and the female proctor turned around at the same time. It was Sara.

'Can you believe it? I have to go, too! How're you doing?'

'Okay, girl, okay – so far!' Max smiled. They rushed down the hall to the ladies' room and stepped into their respective stalls. When Max flushed the toilet, she heard a choking sound. It became a strangled gurgle, and then there was a crash. She hurriedly fastened her jeans and opened the stall door. The proctor was lying on the floor. She was jerking all over like she was having a seizure. It stopped suddenly. She didn't move.

Sara exited her stall a second later. 'What do we do?' she cried.

Max thought quickly. At CMH she had learned that the first thing to check in CPR was the airway. Was she breathing? 'Check her breathing!'

Sara put her ear to the woman's mouth. 'I can't hear anything!'

'Check to see if you can find a pulse,' Max ordered. 'I'll pull her head back and see if there's anything in her throat!' She bent the neck back gently and opened the woman's mouth. With her index and middle fingers she searched the woman's mouth for any obstructions, making sure the tongue was not back in her throat. She even tried to peer down the woman's throat. Nothing.

'I don't think she's breathing!' Sara said in a panic. She was groping for the woman's wrist. 'I can't find a pulse. Max, I don't even know *how* to find a pulse! I've tried on myself, and I never seem to have one!'

'Nothing in her mouth here, either,' Max said to herself. 'All right, listen to me. I'm going to breathe into her mouth. You put your hands on her chest like this, over her heart, like you've seen those ambulance guys and the doctors doing at the hospital, and press and count, saying *one thousand* between each number to keep a rhythm.'

'Gotcha! This I remember!' Sara positioned her hands, one atop the other, and began to press and count.

'Put your whole weight on her!' Max pinched the woman's nose closed. *I hope she isn't sick with something contagious*, she thought as she put her mouth over the woman's and began to puff air into her lungs.

A minute or so passed. Max was winded and Sara was getting tired, but there was no response from the woman.

'Breathe! Breathe! Breathe!' Sara yelled.

'Let's switch,' Max said.

'Can you?' Sara replied, referring to Max's injured arm while crouching next to the woman on the floor to take over the breathing.

'It aches, but forget it!' Max tossed off her jacket and pumped the woman's chest, sweat pouring off her.

'She's not responding, Max! What do we do?' Sara bent down again to puff.

'I'll keep trying to get her to breathe, and I'll alternate pressing on my own,' Max said. 'You run and go get another proctor – no! Forget that! I saw a phone right outside. Call 911!'

'Are you sure?' Sara cried.

Max just nodded and bent down to puff five times then press five times. Puff five times, then press five times.

Sara ran out of the bathroom. Max pressed and puffed, pressed and puffed. The woman still did not move. Three minutes had gone by. Frustrated, Max started to simply pound real hard on the woman's chest. 'Come on! Breathe, damn you! Breathe!' she yelled.

As if the woman had heard her, she coughed.

'Oh, please keep breathing!' Max pleaded with her as she continued to pound on the woman's chest.

Sara raced back in. 'They're on their way! I called them. I just—'

The woman vomited.

'Help me turn her on her side so she doesn't choke!' Max yelled.

Sara pushed from the back while Max held the woman's head and wiped the vomit from her mouth. The woman heaved again. Max held her.

'She's breathing!' Sara said.

They waited for her to stop vomiting and Sara got some more paper towels to wipe up her face and the floor area near her head. That's when they noticed the blood. 'Oh – her head, Max!' Sara whispered.

Max looked at the back of the woman's head. 'She must have cracked it when she fell. What do we do?'

Sara was silent. She pulled off her sweatshirt. 'Give me your shirt, Max!'

Max lowered the woman's head to the floor and handed over her shirt, which left her only in a black tank top. Sara wrapped Max's shirt around the woman's head and tied it on her forehead like a turban. She then wrapped her own sweatshirt into a pillow and placed it under the woman's head. The woman groaned.

'Where are they?' Max said.

'Soon, soon.' Sara breathed deeply, looking around her. 'Aren't we supposed to keep her warm or something?'

'With what?' Max saw nothing they could use

besides her jacket, which she gently placed on top of her.

They waited, watching the woman's chest rise and fall, thankful that she was alive at all. The shirt on her head was getting saturated with blood. The siren of a nearing ambulance sounded outside.

'Go out to the parking lot and see if you can lead them here,' Max said. 'There's nothing else we can do!' Max sat there on the cold floor, holding the woman's hand and telling her, 'You'll be okay. Just keep breathing. The ambulance will be here any second. You'll be okay.'

A minute later Sara returned. She had a blanket over her shoulders and the paramedics were right behind her with a stretcher. 'You did the right thing, girls,' a paramedic said as he leaned over the woman and began to check her vital signs. 'Joe, she's got a skull fracture. We've got to get her on the road.'

They slid a backboard under the woman and attached a cervical collar around her neck. Then, at the count of three, they hoisted her onto the stretcher, placed the oxygen mask over her mouth, and asked Sara to open the door.

Max and Sara stood aside as they rushed the woman out to the ambulance. 'We're taking her to Westside Medical,' the first paramedic called over his shoulder.

'Make way, folks, it's all over,' he said as he pushed through the crowd which had gathered outside the bathroom.

Max suddenly felt a cold panic hit her blood. The test. She was screwed.

'Man, oh, man, that was a close call,' she said quietly.

'No kidding,' replied Sara. 'I hope she makes it.'

Max was silent.

'Hey, you were great in there,' Sara said, nudging her.

'Yeah, but the test . . . I didn't finish the test.'

Sara didn't say anything and Max knew it was because the test was not vital for Sara. Sara had already taken it and was just trying to improve her scores.

'Let's go talk to the proctors.'

Max nodded and followed Sara back to the room, but it was empty. The proctors were gone. Max was filled with quiet desperation.

'Look, Max, you'll get a waiver or something. They can't exactly blame us for this,' Sara said. 'I mean, we should get extra points for the proctors not paying attention! Why didn't the others come out and find us?'

'Maybe they just forgot,' Max replied. After all, there were hundreds of people in that room. Why should one girl trying fervently to get into college matter? In the grand scheme of things, what was one more year of waiting?

Just one more year of my life, Max thought glumly. *That's all.*

8

'Hey, Dagger!'

Dagger turned around. It was Kyle, and he was racing in from the parking lot, pulling on his volunteer shirt. Dagger slowed down to wait for him, trying to shrug the ache out of his shoulders. Charlie Childs, the guy who had offered him a carpentry job with his construction company, Moving Up, was working him harder than he had ever worked in his life. All day on the weekends and every day after school, Dagger was working on a construction site downtown. He was hammering and sawing, lifting, and even digging. He had aches in muscles he didn't remember from science class. He ached from his skull down to the rubber bottoms of his sneakers.

And if that wasn't enough, Gran Tootie made him take up Mr Childs on his offer to tutor him for school. So twice a week the guy came over to his house. Gran Tootie, against the advice of her doctors, cooked up a storm, even though she hadn't even been home for two weeks. Dagger was glad to have her back safe and well, but every night he just had time to shower and eat and then she'd make him sit for hours and study like he'd never studied before. Even his brain hurt! It seemed like his life had turned into pure drudgery in one short week. But at least it kept his mind off the Icers trial. Although the trial had been going on for almost two weeks already, he and Gran Tootie had not been called to testify yet.

'You hear about Max and Sara?' Kyle asked breathlessly, catching up to Dagger.

'Hear what?' Dagger had no idea what Kyle was talking about.

'They're famous, man! They were at the SAT on Saturday—'

Dagger interrupted him. 'The college test Max took? She do really good on it or what?'

'Yeah! No! They went to the test all right, but when they were in the bathroom, some lady hit the floor, had a seizure or something, and stopped breathing. Max and Sara saved her life! The doctors on the news said—'

'They were on the news?' Dagger could not believe he hadn't heard about this. Maybe it was time to start watching the news once in a while, to keep up on stuff. Not like he had the time anymore. *Just what did I used to do with all my time?* he suddenly wondered.

'They were interviewed for the paper and everything. And the doctors on TV said that if it hadn't been for their quick thinking that the lady – she was one of the test proctors – might have been brain damaged! They actually got her to breathe again.' Kyle was totally excited.

'So they're heroes now?' Dagger felt a warmth inside of him. That Max was something else. Too bad she had dumped him. All of a sudden Dagger felt jealous. Max was on the news. That meant that other guys were going to be asking her out, trying to be around her now that she was a big shot. The thought made him feel bad, real bad. He shook his head. 'That girl was still messing up his mind!

'Have you talked to them lately? Since last week?' Dagger asked, trying to sound casual even though he was fishing for news about Max.

'Me? No. I mean, I don't usually talk to them outside the hospital,' replied Kyle. 'Why? You hear anything I should know?'

'No.' Kyle had missed the point altogether. Dagger wanted information!

'Did you go out with that new girl?' Kyle asked.

Dagger looked down at Kyle. Why was Kyle so

interested in his love life? 'No. I didn't really have time, with working and all. So we're going to try to meet this weekend. Tomorrow maybe. It's my only free night!' Dagger couldn't believe that was true. He used to spend every night out. And Gran wasn't letting him off of church on Sundays. She didn't care that he had to be at work at nine; she made him go to early services! Now with work and school and volunteering, he had no time to breathe, much less have a girlfriend. Then it hit him – this was probably what Max was talking about when she said she didn't have any time to fool around when they were together. He had taken it as personal rejection. Now he suddenly realized that she was simply busy with trying to get on with her life and get somewhere.

'Come on, it's almost six,' Dagger mumbled, walking toward Ms Dominguez's office.

Sara and Max were already in there. 'You should have seen her! She was quick! I swear, without Max that woman wouldn't be alive!' Sara was gushing.

'I'm proud of you, Ms Camacho,' Ms Dominguez said. 'You too Ms Greenberg. It sounds to me like you two really came through in a pinch. Now how are you feeling otherwise, Ms Camacho? Are you ready to get back to work? How's that arm? And are you sure you feel emotionally ready to face the ER again?'

'The arm's fine,' Max said. 'That's not what I'm worried about. Actually, I could really use that recommendation from you now, especially since I never finished the test'

'Won't the testing service take the special circumstances into account?' asked Ms Dominguez.

'I spent a lot of time on the phone just trying to explain what happened. At first, they said that it didn't matter if I didn't finish the test – they'll just remove the entire thing from my record. They said they could refund my money or apply it to another test date because I can always take it again – but the next one isn't for a month or so and it's all the way in San Diego. There's no way I can get down there. Then they told me to call back in a week or so. As far as explaining to the colleges why I won't have test scores on time, that's up to me,' Max replied. 'I guess I'll wait until after I hear from them before I start calling any schools.'

'Hmmm,' Ms Dominguez said. 'Doesn't seem fair.'

'Tell me about it,' Sara grumbled. 'It's a total bureaucracy. Oh, hi, Kyle. Dagger.'

'There you are, Mr Cullen. Hello, Mr Fredericks,' Ms Dominguez said. 'Why don't you three go see Nancy in Admitting? Would you please stay in my office, Mr Cullen?'

Kyle grimaced as Dagger and the other volunteers left Kyle in the coordinator's office.

'You know why he's in trouble?' Dagger asked Max, trying to engage her in conversation.

Max looked at him funny. 'How should I know? I wasn't here last week!'

Dagger felt like she had slapped him with the tone of her voice. What was the problem? Was she blaming him for the stabbing? He hadn't had a chance to talk to her since she had gone home from the hospital because her parents had forbidden her contact with him. But her reaction to him was worse than he had expected. Just as Dagger was deciding whether or not to try to pull Max aside, a woman came running in holding her face. 'Help me! Help me! My eye!'

Nancy rushed over to her. The woman's hands were covered with blood. Red stains ran from her chest to her feet. Nancy slowly pulled her hands away from her face, but the woman kept yelling at her, 'Careful! Don't drop it! Careful!'

Dagger saw Nancy's back stiffen. 'Sara, get Dr Milikove on the phone, please,' she said softly. 'Use the loudspeaker.' Dagger knew that was shorthand for: *no time to wait for a response to a beeper page.*

Sara moved swiftly to the phones and paged Dr Milikove over the loudspeaker. Dagger leaned in and nearly got sick at what he saw. The woman was holding one of her eyeballs in her hand. It seemed to be hanging from her eye socket by a few threads, about an inch down on her face. It was like a horror movie. He could not believe what he was seeing.

The woman was babbling. 'I was setting up this chemistry set thing for my son before he got home from baseball and somehow the thing blew up and then the garage caught on fire and I just ran. See I live a block away and I just – oh, please! Can you fix it?'

Dr Milikove raced into the ER. He stood in front of the woman. 'Can you look at me?'

Dagger held his breath.

'No! Not *that* eye, the other one!' Dr Milikove said gruffly.

How was it possible that the eye hanging . . . ? Dagger didn't even want to know. But Dr Milikove sure could work on his bedside manner, Dagger thought. Man, he wasn't very nice. After all, the chick had an eyeball hanging from her face; the least he could do was not scream at her!

'Volunteer! Help me get her onto a gurney! Now! Chop chop!' Dr Milikove ordered Dagger.

Dagger helped the woman onto the gurney and stood back as Nancy asked Max to glove up and attend Dr

Milikove in case he needed help. Sara followed. Nancy gave Dagger an apologetic look. *So everyone knows what a jerk Milikove is*, Dagger noted.

Kyle came over and stood behind Dagger until Nancy asked him to make sure the Trauma Rooms were restocked and had all their supplies. She sent Dagger to the patient waiting room to fill out missing information on a patient chart. *Not again*, he thought. *I did enough admitting duty last week! Please let the guy speak English this time!*

Dagger looked at the chart. It read: *Miss Penny Simonson*. After her name there was a series of question marks and the word *alias*. The chart was otherwise empty. Dagger knew what an alias was, but he didn't know why it was on this chart.

'Miss Simonson?' Dagger called out.

'Shhhh!' came a female voice from the corner.

Dagger walked over to her. She was about forty, dressed in a bright pink suit, and wearing a beanie with a propeller on top of it. She was cradling what looked like a very swollen wrist. 'Ma'am, I need some information from you,' Dagger said politely.

'I can't tell you,' she whispered.

Dagger was stumped. 'What about your address?' he tried.

'Can't tell you that, either,' she hissed. 'Top secret.'

'Insurance information?' he asked, eyebrows raised.

'Oh, no. No, no, no, no, no.' She shook her head adamantly. 'If I do, they might take me away again. Can't have that now, can we?'

She was clearly wacko, but Dagger also knew he could be persuasive if he had to be. Besides, Nancy would kill him if he couldn't get a simple task done like filling out patient information. 'How exactly do you spell your last name?' he asked.

'Simonson, just like it sounds, young man. But that's just my humanoid name. And you can't trick me. For all I know you could be one of them. And if they beam me up again and use me for any more experiments before this last one wears off, I might lose my propeller. And that wouldn't be a pretty picture now, would it?'

'No, ma'am, it sure wouldn't,' Dagger agreed, eyeing the propeller on her cap. 'Just what kind of experiment happened to your wrist there? It is your wrist that's hurt, isn't it?'

'Very astute of you. It was a simple struggle. Mr Spock was trying to steal my ears off me. You know, his are very deformed and he's simply dying for replacements. But I fought him off. I told him that he couldn't have my ears. My ears are mine!' she whispered. 'I happen to have very lovely ones, don't you think?'

'Yes, ma'am, very nice,' Dagger said, pretending to examine them. 'Well, I guess I'll just let the doctors know that you are here. You aren't hurting too bad, are you?'

'No, I'm just fine, young man,' she assured him. 'I can wait here for as long as I have to. I've been trained. I have all eternity to wait in this humanoid disguise. Don't you worry!'

'I won't,' Dagger promised. *Man, this job is too weird.* He was about to go back to Nancy when someone caught his eye. It was Kyra, the beautiful girl from last Friday night in the ER. She had called him twice at home that week, but he had been too busy to call back. 'Hey! What're you doing here?'

'I came to see you,' she stated. 'I looked for you in school, but I didn't see you. And when you didn't call me back, I got worried. Then I remembered you told me you volunteered every Friday night.'

'You remembered?' Dagger was flattered. He sat down next to her. 'So how you been? How's your friend Johnny?'

'He's fine, I guess. He had to go to the police station, and they're going to send him to a reform school for boys outside the city. That guy wasn't dead after all – just knocked out. Johnny's mom is doing okay. That's all I know. I just came by to see if you still wanted to go out tomorrow night like we planned last week.'

Dagger was blown away. This totally fine girl went out of her way to find him and make sure they were still going out? He was floored. 'Sure we're still going out. Oh, listen, I know you called me, but I was at work and then I had to study. Tell you what. I'll tell you where I work during the week. It's near school.' He could just imagine the respect he'd get from the other guys at the site once they saw this babe. They'd stop treating him like a squirt and treat him like the man he was!

She nodded. 'Cool! You were so great to us last week. I knew you were a nice guy.'

Dagger couldn't believe his good fortune. 'Here, let me go get a piece of paper.' Dagger ran over to Nancy's desk, grabbed a piece of message paper, and ran back. 'I'm at work every day from three-thirty till five-thirty – but that's during the week. Tomorrow I get off at five. We could hang, see a movie. Maybe go dancing? I'll call you when I get in.'

'That would be great!' she said. She wrote down her number again for him and he gave her the address of the construction site. When she stood up, she threw her arms around him. Dagger was taken by surprise. 'I just wanted to thank you for helping us and all!' she said sincerely.

Dagger didn't usually respond to big emotional displays, but he hugged her back. Big mistake. There was Max, back from the hanging-eyeball patient, looking like he had just ripped her heart out of her chest and squeezed it to pieces.

'See you!' called Kyra as she skipped out the door.

Dagger tried to smile, but he felt like a total jerk. He was about to go after Max to explain, but as usual, Sara appeared at exactly the wrong time. In a split-second Sara saw what was going on and immediately whisked her friend away.

Dagger shuffled through the admitting charts, looking for the next patient. Well, what did they expect? Max dumped him and now he was supposed to stay away from women for the rest of his life? Dagger felt like hell, so he figured he might as well go help Kyle in the supply closet since things couldn't possibly get much worse.

'Hey, Kyle,' Dagger said. 'Ms Dominguez make you do this again?'

Kyle looked up as he came in. 'For the rest of my tenure here, I have to volunteer for supply restocking if there is ever a need. Worse than that I may have to take this seminar in time management in a few weeks. The only cool thing is that I get to do a double shift tonight.'

Dagger was horrified. 'Cool? A double shift and you're psyched?'

'Think about it, man,' Kyle said. 'The supply cabinet will be completely filled, so I can't possibly do that all night. Plus, I'll get to be alone in the ER during the graveyard shift. That's when all the totally gruesome stuff comes in!'

Dagger thought Kyle was completely nuts. He didn't even know how to respond to such a ridiculous statement. Dagger was the only one of the four who had been assigned to volunteer duty at CMH. He wasn't there by choice, but as penance for petty theft and as an alternative to jail time. So to hear Kyle getting excited about doing twelve hours in one stretch was beyond his comprehension.

'Did you get Max to tell you about everything that happened at the test?' Kyle asked.

'No . . . uh, listen, you got any copies of those newspaper articles about Max and Sara?'

'Actually, I saved them in case . . . oh, I don't know,' Kyle replied. 'I cut them out of the paper. Why?'

'Could I maybe see them? I kind of wanted to read them.'

Kyle looked surprised. 'Sure. I've got them in my locker. You can look at them tonight, if you want.'

Dagger thanked him and walked back to the patient

waiting room to fill out some more charts from Nancy. Miss Simonson winked at him and made a zipper-your-mouth motion at him as he passed by her. He nodded conspiratorially. *Don't you worry, Miss Alien, I won't tell anyone your little secret.* The ER, Dagger had noticed, was filled with weirdos. Unfortunately, not all of them were patients!

9

Sara saw Kyle walk out of the supply closet pushing a cart piled high with towels and scrubs. She followed him into Trauma Room Two. 'Have you heard anything about that girl, Carrie, with the torn aorta from last week?' she asked.

Kyle wiped his long bangs out of his eyes. She noticed that his eyes looked lighter than ever under the glare of the klieg lights. 'No. Maybe we should scope it out later. During break.'

'Fine by me,' she said.

'So I heard about your good deed last Saturday. Pretty impressive,' he said admiringly.

Sara felt her face get hot. 'Well, it wasn't like we had much choice. Max deserves all the credit. She was the one who knew CPR. And she did it with her hurt arm and all.'

'Yeah, but she couldn't have done it alone. I read all about it in the paper. I even saw you on the news when they came by your house,' Kyle said.

'Pretty bizarre, huh? My dad was totally freaked out.' Sara smiled and so did Kyle.

'Was it hard to talk into a camera?' asked Kyle.

'Yes, but they ask you questions and let you try again if you mess up because it's not live or anything. I did wish I had known not to wear yellow, though. I looked kind of dead when I saw it on the news that night,' Sara said.

'I thought you looked great,' Kyle said.

Sara didn't know how to respond so she just ignored his compliment. 'Anyway, the woman is fine. I even spoke to her on the phone! She also called Max, to thank her.'

'What I wouldn't give to be on TV – just once!' Kyle said enviously.

'You'd feel totally different if you were there, Kyle.'

'No way,' he replied. 'I'd be hamming it up. I'd definitely make all my friends watch it!'

Sara shook her head. It hadn't been like that at all. He had no idea.

Kyle finished piling the scrubs on the rack outside the Trauma Room and rolled the empty cart back toward the supply closet.

'You on supply duty?' she asked.

'Permanently,' he replied. 'Ms D. really let me have

it for slacking off on the schedule last week. I got this as a sort of probation. Plus, I have to take this seminar in a few weeks on time management. A whole weekend day. But I did get an extra shift. That's not like a punishment or anything. I think she's trying to test me to see if I can hack it like a med student with no sleep.'

Sara looked up to see Ms Dominguez coming toward them. 'See you!' Kyle whispered and pushed the cart quickly away.

Sara watched him disappear into the supply closet. She sort of wished she could go in there with him and keep talking. More and more, even though she talked to him often, Sara was starting to feel farther away from Josh. Not that she didn't care about him – that wasn't it at all. They had just somehow become more like friends than boyfriend-girlfriend. When they talked, it felt like brother and sister. She still missed all the closeness, but lately she was beginning to wonder if she was missing *Josh*, or just a boyfriend in general.

'Sara!' Nancy's voice rocked her from her thoughts. 'I need you to go over to the pathology lab to get results on a culture.' She handed Sara a piece of paper. Except for the lady with the eyeball, the night in the ER seemed pretty calm so far. Too calm.

Sara made her way into the basement of the hospital where the pathology lab was located. Right next to

94

the blood lab, it was a huge area with big metal tables covered with microscopes and beakers standing in white plastic trays. Plastic cultures were kept in refrigerators under the tables. Techs using eyedroppers pulled out droplets of whatever was in the cultures and plopped them onto slides that were carefully inched under microscopes. For a Friday night, the place was pretty busy.

Sara rang the bell at the front desk and a tech came over to assist her. The results Nancy wanted would not be ready for another fifteen minutes. Did she want to wait or be called upstairs when it was ready? Sara told them she'd be right back.

She was feeling hungry so she opted to stop by the locker room and get some of her favorite cookies out of her locker. When she rummaged in her backpack, a piece of paper came out stuck to the cellophane. It was a phone number – the number her mother had written her in the letter she had sent Sara. It was in Arizona. She had written that Sara could call anytime, collect.

Sara pulled a cookie out of the wrapping and sat nibbling on it, staring at the piece of paper. She had let a week go by since she had decided that she might call her mom. She still wasn't sure if she really wanted to, so she had purposely waited – especially considering the last time she had corresponded with her. Now she regretted sending such a mean, rejecting letter. She wished she had been more mature. She couldn't really ask her dad about what he, as an adult, would have thought receiving a letter like that from a daughter, because if her dad knew that her mother had contacted her in the first place, he would blow his top. And she couldn't really ask Max because Max didn't know the whole truth about Sara's problems with her mother. Dagger knew, but Sara couldn't really talk to him about much lately because of his current situation with Max. She had even considered telling Ms Dominguez about it, but then she decided that was too personal to share with someone who was like a boss. If Ms Dominguez found out about her screwed-up family life, she might look at Sara differently, and Sara couldn't bear that. So she just continued to second-guess what was going on in her mother's head. Someday she might actually talk to her. Someday. But she felt so guilty about it all, even though it was her mother who was the jerk all her life. God! She felt so bad all the time about it!

'Hey! What's up?' Max's voice came crashing through Sara's head, startling her.

'Nothing,' Sara said quickly. Then she burst into tears.

Max rushed over. 'What's wrong, Sara? What is

it?' Sara sobbed on Max's shoulder for what seemed like an eternity.

'Tell me. You'll feel better, really,' Max urged.

'It's – my mother.' Everything came pouring out. 'Max, there's so much you don't know. When I was little, she used to drink. She beat me all the time. I was always afraid of her.' Sara paused. 'She wrote me a letter a few weeks ago. I wrote back a really mean one. I just feel so bad, but I don't want to call her – not really. I mean, sometimes I do, but then I feel like she's controlling me! And I won't let her do that again! I won't! That's all.'

'Oh, is that all?' Max said, trying to lighten things up even though her mind was racing with what she had just heard. Suddenly it was clear to her why Sara was so sensitive to children's injuries! 'Well, just think of it this way: At least you can fit her letter into a trash can. Dagger's too tall.'

Sara laughed despite herself and wiped her face with her sleeve. They got up and began to walk back toward the lab. 'Oh, Max, what is it lately? First you getting stabbed, then Josh leaving, then that woman at the SAT . . . Between you and me, we seem to have cornered the market in bad luck.'

'No kidding,' Max said. 'What are you going to do? Are you really not going to call your mom ever?'

'No! Yes! I don't know! It seems like ever since I got that letter from her, I've been nervous about her again. I used to want her to call or write so badly that I could feel this little pit in my stomach all the time. I don't anymore. I had six years of relative peace. I'm fine without her. Next year I'll be leaving for college, and I'll get to start a whole new life. I'm just not sure that I want her in it now!'

'What if she's really sorry?' Max asked. 'What if she's really changed?'

'Fat chance,' Sara said. 'My dad said she used to write to him to ask for money when she had drunk all hers up. Can you believe that? She . . . just . . . left!' She felt her eyes well up again. 'And if she thinks I'm going to *listen* to *anything* she has to say – well – she can forget it!' Sara got up to go back to the lab and Max followed her.

Sara could tell Max was feeling pretty miserable, as well. She started to feel selfish. After all, it was Max's first night back after she had been stabbed! She shouldn't be bothering Max with all her problems. 'Listen, Max, forget Dagger. He's a snake. He has no right to be going out with other girls – so soon, anyway,' Sara added.

'Not true! We're not together anymore,' Max said strongly. 'It's not fair for me to insist that he stay alone. It's just that I had no idea he'd recover so quickly, you know what I mean?'

'You wish he'd have suffered a little longer, right?' Sara said sympathetically.

Max nodded miserably. 'Exactly.' Then Max tried to change the subject. 'But you still haven't told me what you're going to do about your mom.'

'Same thing you're doing about Dagger right now – nothing!' Sara replied. 'We better get back to work. Come on. I'll bring my cookies and we can drown our sorrows in high-fat content and empty calories.'

'Sounds good to me!'

10

Kyle had told everyone who asked about the conse-
quences of his meeting with Ms Dominguez, but he
had left out one little detail – the one that could ruin
all his chances to be a doctor. Ms Dominguez had
threatened to withhold his college recommendation
if he didn't shape up. Her actual parting words to him
earlier that evening were pretty harsh: '*If you slip up
again, you can kiss this program good-bye. I am a
volunteer coordinator, not your mother. I don't have
to give you another chance.*'

Kyle continued stacking supplies on the cart. He
felt like a player kicked off the team. Everyone else
was in the game; he had to sit on the bench. He pushed
the last load of supplies into cubicle twenty-four and
unloaded them slowly, feeling sorry for himself.

On his way back toward the admitting desk, he
watched in amazement as two teenagers stumbled into
the room, lurching oddly sideways. They were stepping

all over each other. They seemed to be connected at the mouth.

Kyle blinked. Were they Siamese twins or something? They kept tripping. Kyle went over to help them at Nancy's desk.

Embarrassed at his own nosiness, he sneaked a glance at their connection point. That's when he saw that they were connected not at the mouth – but at the teeth! Their braces were locked together. Scads of drool dripped unchecked from their open mouths.

Kyle felt a surprised chuckle pop out of his mouth. Both of the teenagers reacted at once.

'Itf not funny!'

'He'v fulling off fy teef!'

'If your fault!'

'Na-ah! I didn't even want to ftart kiffing!'

'Hey!' Kyle interrupted the bickering teenage couple. 'Listen, we'll get you unhooked in a minute. Just sit down in here and wait, okay? I've got to get some admitting papers for you.'

The two teenagers glared at one another and sideways at Kyle, allowing themselves to be led into the cubicle.

Kyle went back to Nancy's desk. She was laughing. 'I took them into a cubicle to, you know, spare them.'

'Spare *them*?' Nancy joked. 'Here.' She handed Kyle

a blank chart and admitting forms. 'See if you can get their names through all that saliva.'

'Fery funny,' he mimicked. He caught a retreating intern leaving another cubicle. 'Got a moment?' he asked. 'We've got a train wreck in cubicle four.'

She looked at him askance and rushed in. He heard her chuckle mightily when she saw the kids. They immediately started bickering again in loud but nonsensical gibberish. 'Volunteer!'

Kyle walked into the cubicle.

'Could you please hold this for me?' The intern was indicating the top lips of the two kids, which she had pulled up away from their braces. The girl was sucking in her breath, trying to keep some of her saliva from dribbling out of her mouth. 'Give it up for now,' the intern instructed her. 'Plenty of time to wipe off later. I need you to be still so I don't stab you with these.' She indicated a small set of clippers.

Kyle held up their lips. The intern went over to the other side. Their four faces were all very close together.

With a quick clip and a snip, the teenagers were separated. They pulled away from one another. The girl immediately started to wipe off her face and check her hair. The boy ran his fingers through his hair in a desperate attempt to appear cool. Their dignity was totally shattered. Kyle felt kind of bad for them. He looked at the intern. She smiled at him and addressed the kids.

'You'll both have to get in to see your orthodontists as soon as possible. I had to snip off a few wires so they wouldn't cut your mouth.'

The kids nodded. The intern must have felt bad because she started to ask the kids their identifying information when she could have just handed Kyle the chart. Kyle knew he should keep busy so he reluctantly walked back into the admitting area in the ER. Sara was seated and talking to a young woman who was so skinny that she looked like a skeleton. Max was out in the patient waiting area. Dagger was hanging up a bunch of newly filled-in patient admissions charts.

Kyle watched Sara. She was asking questions and the teenage girl's head was lowered. The tendons in her neck stood out like ropes and her face was all bones and blue veins. Kyle noticed that Sara's hands were shaking on the papers she was holding in her lap. He wondered what was wrong with the girl, but before he had the chance to even think about it, the doors to the ambulance bay slammed open and two fire department paramedics rushed in with what looked to Kyle like an empty stretcher.

'Trauma Three,' Nancy instructed them. 'Dagger,

go with them. Kyle, you follow. Be there to run any errands if needed.'

Kyle winced. So Ms Dominguez must have told Nancy that he was now the Useless-Errands Boy. Great. From Mr Potential Doctor to Supply Boy. Kyle followed as Dagger led the way into the Trauma Room. Dr Milikove and a nurse were already at the side of the stretcher.

'What have we got?' the doctor asked.

'Infant, four months old. Not breathing. We've got her on oxygen, but she's not pulling on her own. Extensive CPR, but nothing.'

'You checked the airways, circ, everything?'

'Yes.'

'Any rhythm?'

'It was irregular when we got there.'

'Defib?'

'Yes. Twice. But then it just went to flatline.'

'How long had she stopped breathing before you got to her?'

'About five minutes. Parents were in a panic. Seems she was just sleeping, she cried out, her mother went in to check on her, she wasn't breathing. We've been working on her the whole way here, but we couldn't resuscitate.'

Kyle winced. The baby was so tiny she looked like

she barely weighed six pounds. She was skinny and helpless in that particularly awful way that infants seemed on stretchers meant for bodies at least ten times their size. He looked up at Dagger, who was just staring at the body.

'Let's try a fluid challenge,' Dr Milikove ordered.

The baby was hooked up to an IV and fluids were injected into the tube to try to start her breathing. The techs checked the infant's reading on the heart monitor, but the reading was still flat. Dagger and Kyle watched as the resuscitation efforts continued.

'Clear!'

Everyone moved back from the table as the infant jerked in response to the electrical current. Dr Milikove checked the EKG monitor. Nothing.

'Again. Clear!'

The baby's body jerked again, but the monitor's line remained flat. They pushed on the chest, trying to force air into her tiny lungs, but the baby did not respond. Machines, people, oxygen – nothing worked.

'We got a straight line, folks.' Dr Milikove removed his mask. 'This one's a code gray. Someone get Child Protective Services in here, have them run down the usual. I want X rays, a CAT scan, and blood work recorded on this. I'll go speak with the parents.'

Connie Rosenfeld, the head trauma nurse, looked

at Dagger and said, 'Pediatric Care Unit. They'll get the on-call Child Protective Services rep down here. You can explain the situation as you understood it and ask her to come down. Okay?' Dagger nodded and Kyle watched him leave to go do his important task.

The nurse then addressed him. 'Get me the portable X-ray machine and a blood tech in here. I don't want to be moving this infant around from room to room in front of the patients. We'll do the tests we can in here. Go!'

Kyle took one last look at the tiny child. Even the techs were silent. Losing a baby was awful. Kyle ran to fetch the machine. He had to go to three different rooms down the hall from the ER before he found an available one. By the time he returned, Dagger was already in the room with the Child Protective Services woman. She was the smallest person Kyle had ever seen who wasn't a kid.

Mrs Conner was so short that she didn't even reach Dagger's waist. She must have been three feet tall. When she turned to the gurney, he was surprised to see a face so wrinkled and tanned that she looked about three hundred years old.

'Mr Fredericks, can you give me the basics?'

Kyle felt left out and unimportant as he watched

Dagger, for once, take over the situation with confidence. Dagger began with a big breath. 'It's a baby girl, four months old. The paramedics said that she was sleeping, she cried out in her sleep, and by the time the parents got to her she was already not breathing. It was about five minutes before the fire department got there. They did CPR but couldn't get her breathing again. They defibrillated before she got to the ER, then in the ER again, and did a fluid challenge. No luck. Dr Milikove called it a code gray.' Dagger finished, clearly proud of the official way he sounded. He looked down at the tiny older woman. She shook her head.

'Too bad for the parents. Dr Milikove mention a specific reason for wanting us up here?' Mrs Conner asked.

'What do you mean, ma'am?' Dagger asked.

'You can call me Mrs Conner,' she ordered. 'I *mean* that we are required to fill out a report on the deaths of all minors. I was wondering, however, if Dr Milikove gave any indication of any suspicions he might have.'

'No, I don't think so,' replied Dagger. 'But why do you have to check up on the deaths of kids and not everyone else?'

'Watch. Listen. And learn. *Before* you ask silly, obvious questions!' she replied loudly. Kyle felt better all of a sudden. 'Now. Where are the parents?' she asked.

'I . . . I don't know, ma – I mean Mrs Conner,' Dagger replied stupidly.

Kyle smiled to himself. 'They're with Dr Milikove in the holding room,' he said smartly.

'Why on earth did he take them in there?' Mrs Conner asked him sharply, as if he were Dr Milikove's puppeteer. The holding room was where criminals with police escorts were held while they were waiting to be treated. It had a lock on the outside. 'Where *is* his head?'

Nancy slipped her head in the door – no doubt because she heard the commotion. 'Anything I can help with, Mrs Conner?' she asked politely. Kyle heard the caution in her cheerful voice. As she repeated her question, Kyle guessed that Mrs Conner must have a temper three times her size.

'You know Dr Milikove,' Nancy answered in a whisper. 'Big brain, bigger britches.' It was Nancy's very nice way of saying that Dr Milikove did not know how to behave.

Mrs Conner snorted and scurried out as the X-ray tech entered to do his business. When the tech was finished, she walked back in and examined the chart. The baby's covered body was still on the gurney. Mrs

Conner lifted the sheet and examined the child. She peered into its eyes and even turned it over. Even in her small hands, the baby looked helplessly tiny.

'Listen to me, young man. Listen and learn.'

Kyle was surprised to hear her addressing Dagger and not him.

'No bruises, no apparent physical traumas, you see?'

Dagger nodded.

'But the X rays and the CAT scan will tell us more,' she continued. 'The blood tests will, too. You see, every once in a while a child actually does die for no apparent reason. It's called SIDS – sudden infant death syndrome. They just stop breathing. Sometimes post-mortem tests show nothing. Sometimes they show that it was the result of a congenital defect that the parents and doctors were not aware of. But sometimes' – here she peered at Dagger out of her wrinkled face – 'a history of bruises or broken bones show up in a very young child. Parents abusing them. Or even poison, suffocation, drowning. I've seen it all. And you never know. That's why we are here. To make sure.'

'But the kid just died! How are you going to talk to the parents? How can you accuse them if you don't really know?' Kyle burst out.

Mrs Conner looked at him as if he were an imbecile. 'I don't *accuse* them of anything, young man. I just

109

ask questions – and I do it very delicately. If the tests indicate reason for suspicion, the hospital files a report and the police and lawyers take over,' Mrs Conner replied. 'Let's go.' She covered up the baby and wrote some notes on the chart. Then she marched out and over to the holding room. Kyle followed Dagger. He didn't want to miss this one. She knocked twice and walked in without being asked. Dagger followed her. Kyle slipped in by the skin of his teeth.

'I'm Mrs Conner,' she said sweetly, standing near the two parents. Her voice had changed from that of a small sergeant to that of a kindly grandmother. Kyle caught Dagger's eye. He was just as surprised at the change. 'And I'm so sorry for your loss,' they heard her say.

The parents were young, in their late twenties or early thirties, Kyle guessed. The woman was weeping and the man was trying to comfort her.

'Did you do everything you could, doctor?' asked the father.

Dr Milikove frowned. 'We and the paramedics administered CPR and did everything in our power to save the patient. Your daughter did not respond. I'm . . . sorry.' It seemed to Kyle that the small comfort of his words had to be wrenched out of Dr Milikove's mouth, as if he found being nice beyond his powers. 'Well, I have other matters to attend to. This woman will answer any other questions you have.' He stood up and abruptly left the room. The father's eyes followed him out, a disbelieving expression on his face.

Mrs Conner jumped in immediately. 'I apologize,' she said gently. 'Some doctors just get so upset that they have a hard time with this.' Kyle knew it was a white lie to make them feel better. 'Before I ask you some questions so we can take care of all of this, would you like something to drink? Some water?'

Both the parents just stared at her.

'You!' she snapped her fingers in Kyle's direction. She indicated the chair he was sitting in, the one Dr Milikove had vacated. He blushed hotly and quickly stood up. He watched her unself-consciously climb into the chair, huffing and puffing throughout the ordeal. When she was situated, her feet dangled a good six inches from the floor.

'Why don't you tell me what happened? I know you've been through this already, but I would really appreciate hearing your version myself,' Mrs Conner said.

The father looked at the mother, who shook her head. He began to recount the story, the same one Kyle had heard from the paramedics.

'How long before you called for help?'

'We called 911 right away when we realized Julie wasn't breathing. But they took so long to arrive!' The father broke down again and Mrs Conner handed him some tissues. 'We tried to breathe into her mouth and even pump her little chest, but—' He sobbed, unable to continue.

'I know, I know, it's terrible,' said Mrs Conner, her voice soothing. 'You!' she indicated Kyle again.

What is it about me? Kyle thought. *Do I have the word* servant *stamped onto my forehead?*

'Two cups of water?' she asked, but it was not a question.

Kyle nodded and slipped out of the room. He went into the kitchen area where the ER doctors and nurses had a refrigerator and a beat-up old sofa and table area in which to inhale nourishment between shifts. He quickly filled two cups with cold water from the dispenser and rushed back toward the holding room, balancing the cups in front of him.

All of a sudden he was covered in water. He had crashed into someone. He looked up slowly into the face of Dr Milikove. Water was dripping from his caterpillar-like monobrow.

'You stupid idiot!' Dr Milikove hissed. 'Can't you watch where you're going? Are you blind or just spastically uncoordinated? What is your—?' He flung his hands down and wiped his face with the edge of his lab coat.

'I . . . I'm sorry!' Kyle stuttered. He was more astonished at the doctor's reaction than anything else. 'I—'

'—don't care what *you* anything!' Dr Milikove interrupted him. 'Damn volunteers. Baby-sitting is all we do for you! We should never allow you brats anywhere near the ER. Damned incompetent! Listen' – he yanked Kyle's ID tag off his shirt so he could read it – 'Cullen! Do us both a favor and stay out of my way!' With that Dr Milikove tossed down Kyle's tag and stormed away.

Kyle slowly leaned down to pick up his drenched tag and clip it back on. As he did he caught sight of Sara's face. She was looking at him in pity. So was the skeletal girl she was talking to. Shoot! It was just *water!* He turned away. He felt so humiliated, he could feel the heat of his face on his wet collar. Had everyone in the entire ER seen Dr Milikove chew him out? When he looked up again, everyone's face was averted except for Nancy's. Yep, everyone had. Even Dagger had seen through the glass window of the holding room. Nancy looked like she was about to speak, but just shook her head and went back to her paperwork.

Kyle grabbed a towel and mopped up the puddle of

water. He then made his way back to the kitchen and refilled two new cups with water. Was this night going to just keep getting worse or what?

11

Max left the patient waiting area and went back into the ER with a pile of admitting forms. She slipped them into the slots on the wall near Nancy's desk. The urgents were patients who had to be seen right away, but those people were usually taken right into a cubicle. The immediates were those who needed care sooner rather than later. Then came the nonurgents, who often had to wait a long time since their injuries were not life-threatening. All of Max's charts this time went into nonurgent slots.

'What was all that yelling?' Max asked Nancy.

Nancy sighed. 'Dr Milikove strikes again. He just ate Kyle half-alive for accidentally spilling water on his precious lab coat.'

'I bet Kyle just loved that!' Max said wryly.

Nancy smiled. 'Let's just say he'll probably be acting a bit more humble tonight.'

'Poor Kyle. He's no match for Dr Milikove,' Max said.

'Who is?' Nancy grabbed the first chart from the immediates. 'Max, take Ms Hilderley into cubicle seven and tell Dr Kopelow she's there.'

Max made her way into the waiting room and called out Ms Hilderley's name. A young woman with a gorgeous halo of blond corkscrew curls hefted herself up out of her chair. She was very pregnant. Max took her elbow and escorted her into the cubicle. 'Have a seat, Ms Hilderley,' Max offered. 'Dr Kopelow will be in here shortly.'

Ms Hilderley smiled wearily. 'Good. I've never had a baby before and I'm a month early, but I swear if this pain isn't labor, then I don't know what is.'

'Did you tell the admitting nurse?' Max asked, alarmed.

'Yes, but she asked me a few questions and said it wasn't urgent, and not to worry. My water's not broken, so I guess . . .' She shrugged her shoulders.

'Okay, don't worry,' Max said. 'The doctor will be in soon.'

'Thanks.'

Max went back to the admitting desk.

'Max, I've got something I want you to do,' Nancy said. 'I can't find any available orderlies, so I need you to take the gurney and the body in Trauma Room Three over to CAT Scan. Then wait there for the test to be done – there's an immediate opening – and make sure the results get back here for Dr Milikove and Mrs Conner to review with the rest of the chart. Then take her down to the morgue.'

Max's eyes flew open. 'Me?'

Nancy's expression was frank. 'Look, it's got to be done. Besides, you've been down there before. At least it's not your first time. And take the staff elevators.'

'What am I, the grim reaper?' Max grumbled good-naturedly, feeling her hunger pangs suddenly subside. Why her? Nancy was right. She had already been down there. It had been during her first or second week of volunteering. Max had been observing an operation in which a young man's feet had been severed in a car accident and they were trying to save his life. When it was determined that the feet could not be reattached, it was Max who had to go down to the morgue. She would never forget carrying the two ice-filled buckets, each holding a once-live foot. She had been petrified, but the morgue was just like a big freezer. There were steel walls filled from floor to ceiling with long drawers that slid open to reveal the bodies. Through a short hallway were two autopsy rooms. But it was the odor that was the worst. It was sterilized in there, but it smelled like the frogs in science class that were kept in jars of formaldehyde. It was gross.

Max lumbered off to Trauma Room Three. She had heard about the baby girl who had been brought in already dead. Max loved kids and didn't want to have to see her at all. She inhaled and entered the room. At first, she couldn't see the body on the gurney because it was so tiny. But then she did. It was a small bump under the sheet. Max thought she could make out the shapes of the baby's round belly and her head.

Yuck! She was about to wheel the gurney out when she stopped and hunted for a blanket. She covered the entire body with the folded blanket so it wouldn't look like there was anything on the gurney. Then she pushed the gurney out the door and down the hall. The CAT scan room was adjacent to the X-ray lab. The CAT scan was a huge machine that looked like a contraption out of a sci-fi movie. A large metal cylinder over six feet long, it had a table that pulled out like a drawer on which the patient was immobilized. It was used to detect soft tissue damage inside the body.

Max checked in with the receptionist who had been waiting for her arrival. Max was glad she did not have to explain. A short while later the body was wheeled out again, this time without the blanket on it, just the sheet.

'Poor baby,' clucked the tech.

The receptionist nodded. 'Shame.'

Max didn't say a word. She wheeled the body out and into a staff elevator. Down a floor and to the right. Max felt a little bit creepy being alone in the deserted halls. It reminded her of the lonely stairwell where she had been stabbed such a short time ago. But she pushed the feeling as far away from her as she could. She could not afford to start freaking out now. At the double steel doors, Max pressed a button to announce her arrival.

A voice came out of the speaker. 'Yes?'

'Volunteer here from ER. I've got an infant.'

'Speak into the speaker. Can't hear you.'

Max repeated herself, louder this time, her mouth nearly touching the plastic box with her lips. Her glance fell on the inert shape under the sheet. *Please don't make me repeat this*, Max prayed silently. *I can't say it again or I'll bust.* Mercifully, the door clicked and Max moved back. The steel doors slid with a lurch as the gap between them widened. Max gulped and pushed the gurney in front of her.

'This the baby they called about?' the tech asked.

'I guess. It's the only one I know about in the ER tonight,' Max replied.

The tech pressed a button to close the steel doors behind Max. Then she lifted the sheet off. 'Oh, what a shame. Poor little girl. What happened?'

'She just stopped breathing, I think,' Max replied.

The tech clucked, slipped on some gloves, and picked up the baby, placing her on a table in the middle of the room. 'Papers?'

Max handed over the papers. 'The rest are coming. I just came from CAT Scan.'

'What about blood work?'

'On its way.' Max watched as the woman began to examine the baby. She averted her eyes. 'Uh, can I go?'

'Sure you don't want to watch? A dead body is like a good mystery. The entire story of a person's life is written somewhere on the body. Some of it we don't fully understand, like what goes on in the brain, but it's all there. We just have to learn how to crack the code.' She looked at Max expectantly.

Max felt a shiver go through her. She knew that if she wanted to be a doctor she'd have to watch autopsies some times. She'd probably even have to do one. But – her eyes slid over to the tiny body on the gurney – she couldn't watch this woman cut up a baby! She just couldn't.

'Nah, I'll pass, thanks,' she said. 'Maybe some other time.' She was trying to be nice. She couldn't understand how this woman could seem to love her work so much. If Max had to do it, she'd probably have horrible nightmares. 'I bet it would be interesting, but—'

'Oh, I understand. Don't you worry,' the technician said. 'Most people have a hard time with death. But me – well, I just see it as a stage in life that we all have to go through sooner or later. You go on. I'll send up a report when I'm done here.'

Max nodded, but for some reason she didn't move – not right away. Instead, she glanced over at the gurney again. The technician seemed pretty sure she could find out what had made the baby stop breathing. Max hoped the baby hadn't been hurt on purpose – suffocated or strangled by her parents. That would be awful beyond belief. But then again, it was awful to think that a tiny baby like this could just die for no obvious reason.

'It's most likely SIDS,' the technician said, her voice cutting into Max's thoughts. 'In cases where there isn't any obvious sign of trauma, like this, that's what it is nine times out of ten.'

'But why? I mean, why would a kid just stop breathing?'

The technician shook her head. 'Most experts today don't think there's any single cause for SIDS. Some researchers think that certain children are born with faulty respiratory regulatory systems. That means that when they're asleep they sometimes just stop breathing for no reason. Others think that SIDS isn't caused by a birth defect, but by a virus – a normal cold virus that somehow interferes with some babies' breathing patterns. SIDS seems to strike low birthweight babies and babies who are bottlefed more frequently. But that's not always who gets the illness. Researchers have learned that children who sleep face down are more likely to die of SIDS. But as for a real cause' – the technician threw up her gloved hands – 'no one knows for sure. Yet.'

'Then how do you know it's SIDS?' Max asked, curious now.

'We make what's called an *exclusionary diagnosis*.'

'A what?'

'We rule out everything else. For example, we check the infant for abrasions, fiber in the throat which might indicate suffocation, any sort of internal injury, or an undiagnosed birth defect – say a malformed heart. If none of these things are there, we can be pretty sure its SIDS.'

Max glanced down at the small body on the table. Despite herself, she was becoming interested in what the woman was telling her. But the morgue still gave her the creeps. Max took a deep breath and almost gagged on the thick, sweetish smell of the formalde-hyde. 'Well,' she said weakly, 'I better get going now.'

The technician waved. 'Sure,' she said. 'You go on. I'll send up a report when I'm done here. It shouldn't be too long. Oh, and tell Chelly if you see her that Selene says hi.'

Max mumbled a good-bye and slunk through the doors as soon as they allowed enough space for her to slide through sideways. She felt incredibly relieved when she was safely out in the hallway. Selene had helped her better understand what took place in the hospital morgue. She could even sort of see why some people liked working there. But she couldn't imagine doing it herself. Performing autopsies in medical school was going to be tough.

At least Selene didn't seem to think that anyone had hurt the baby on purpose. In a way that was a comfort, but in another way it wasn't. *The poor parents,* Max thought. *Imagine having a healthy baby one day and the next* . . . Max sighed.

She stopped back in the CAT scan room to make sure the records were to go directly up to the ER and be delivered into Nancy's hands. On the way back to the ER, she suddenly started thinking about Dagger again.

Max had told Sara that Dagger had a perfect right to go out with other girls if he wanted. Still, that didn't mean she felt happy about it. How could Dagger have a new girlfriend already? Even though Max hadn't really felt threatened when she first heard about it, now she realized she hated the idea. Sara was sure that it was harmless. *Maybe*, Max thought. But now that he was flaunting the new girl in front of her at the hospital, it was too humiliating to be believed. *How did I go from being pretty sure I wanted to break up with him to feeling like I was the one who was dumped?* she wondered.

And the worst part was that she still liked him. She felt like an idiot, but it was the truth. She had seen a sweetness in Dagger unlike anything else she had ever experienced. Underneath that macho exterior, he was a really nice guy, and fun to be around.

It was all just so complicated. And now, with her college future in jeopardy because of the unfinished SAT, Max didn't know what to do about anything. Why was it that everything always seemed to happen at once?

When she reached the ER, Nancy had her wheel Ms Hilderley up to Maternity. The patient's water had broken, and she was now officially in labor – a month early. Ms Hilderley clenched Max's hand so hard that she found it difficult to wheel the gurney.

'Am I going to be okay?' she pleaded, her blond curls falling across her face. She looked terrified.

'Of course you are,' Max said soothingly. Then she crossed her fingers, hoping it was true.

She left Ms Hilderley in Maternity and took the elevator back down to the ER. As she came in, the EMS computer screeched. There was a call coming in from an ambulance. Nancy pressed the speaker button.

'CMH, this is EMS one-forty-two. Do you read?'

'EMS one-forty-two, this is CMH. What have you got?'

'Female, one-eight to two-oh, in severe respiratory crisis. We went out in response to an emergency call, but when we got there she wasn't breathing. We resuscitated. She's awake and on oxygen. Out.'

'EMS one-forty-two, what is your ETA?'

'Two minutes, CMH. We're around the corner. And we advise precaution upon arrival. Patient has full-blown AIDS. Out.'

Nancy jotted this last bit of information down. Then the speaker activated again.

'CMH, this is EMS one-forty-two. By the way, we've got an unattended toddler with us. Appears healthy but scared. We think it might be her son. There was no other adult on the premises. Do you copy?'

Nancy's concern showed on her face. 'EMS one-forty-two, we copy. Out.'

Max was startled. She wondered if this kind of thing happened all the time. What *did* you do if you had to take a patient to the hospital and there were kids there? Was it usual to just bring them along? Nancy interrupted her thoughts.

'Glove up, Max, and tell anyone else going into Trauma Room Two to do the same. Then I want you to slide the biohazard card into the slot on the door to warn any of the doctors as well. You have to be careful with AIDS patients, their secretions, and their medical waste. Then I want you to find another volunteer to go with you. Someone's going to have to watch the kid until I get someone else from Child Protective Services down here. Mrs Conner is still busy with the infant girl's parents.'

'Have they found out what happened to the baby yet?' Max asked. She knew it wasn't any of her business – not really – but she couldn't help wanting to know.

'Selene just submitted a preliminary report,' Nancy replied quietly. 'It looks like SIDS. The CAT scan and blood work seem to confirm it.'

'That's too bad,' Max said. She was thinking that it must have made it even worse for the parents to know they were being suspected of causing their child's death. Most likely they were so upset they hadn't even noticed.

'Yes, it is,' Nancy said. 'It's another one of those

things that happen that just don't seem fair.' She looked up at Max. 'You should go,' she prodded gently. 'That ambulance is going to be here any minute.'

Max nodded and ran to put the sign up on Trauma Room Two. The first volunteer she caught sight of was Dagger. Damn! 'Dagger, Nancy wants you to help me here.'

Dagger paused and then walked over to her. He had an annoying grin on his face. 'At your service.'

'Knock it off,' she snapped. 'Come on. Let's go to the ambulance bay. There's an AIDS patient coming in and she has a kid with her.'

They were outside in the cold night air. They could see the lights of an ambulance pulling up the ramp into the bay. The lights were shut off and the wagon backed into the space. Its back doors were thrown open and an EMS tech jumped out and turned to pull out the stretcher while another EMT held it at the other end. Then the driver popped out and went into the wagon from the open back doors. He seemed to be talking to someone. *It's probably the kid*, Max thought.

She turned to look at the face on the stretcher. The young woman looked so familiar. Her arms were covered with the purple bruises of Kaposi's sarcoma that plagued a great many AIDS patients, and she was so slender that her face was totally buried under the oxygen mask. Max couldn't figure out just what she recognized, and then the stretcher was whisked into the ER. She moved toward the back of the ambulance, and peered in. There, in the glare of the lights inside the large space of the wagon, crouched a little boy, eyes large and frightened. Max's hand flew to her mouth.

It was Ricardito, Teresa's little boy!

12

Dagger saw Max's reaction and looked in. He couldn't see anything except the ambulance driver's back.

'What's wrong, Max?' he whispered.

'It's Ricardito. Remember that girl our age who came when we first volunteered? The Hispanic one with AIDS?' Max said, eyes still intent on the inside of the ambulance.

Dagger couldn't remember half the people *he* talked to in the ER, much less all the ones Max had talked to. 'Yeah. Why?'

'Well, she's back. Again. She was here about a month ago, too. You know – I had to watch her kid when she was here that time. She must be real sick. And she doesn't have any family or a husband to care for her son so he's going to have to be put in a foster home. Wait, shhhh.' Max moved in front of him and addressed the ambulance driver's back. 'I . . . uh, I know this kid. Can I try?'

The driver looked at her and moved back. 'Go ahead. He's scared to death!'

Dagger watched as Max pulled herself up into the wagon. He could hear her voice, soothing and sweet. 'Hi, Ricky! Remember me? I'm your mom's friend.'

The boy looked up when she said his name. For a moment, he looked like he might even allow her to take him out. A few weeks ago he had known her by name! But his face clouded up again. Could he have forgotten her so fast? His experience in the ambulance must have really shaken him up.

Max spoke to him in Spanish. '*Ven conmigo, Ricardito. Vamos a comer una galleta en la cocina. Ven!*' Max held out her hand.

Dagger had no idea what Max had said, but the little boy did. He smiled and reached up his hands. Max unbuckled him from the seat and pulled him into her arms, crooning to him gently and hugging him close to her body. She came out of the back of the wagon and headed into the ER.

Dagger followed Max and the boy to Nancy's desk. 'Nancy, this is the little boy who came in here with his mom a few weeks ago. Remember?'

Nancy studied the little boy who promptly hid his face shyly in Max's shirt. 'Wasn't his mom's brother in here a while back for an industrial accident of some sort? A finger sliced?' Nancy paused, racking her brains. 'Hector?'

Dagger was impressed. Thousands of people came into CMH every week. It was the nation's busiest public hospital, and yet Nancy could remember who was who!

'Right!' Max said. 'Teresa was just brought in here again. She's the AIDS patient.' Before Nancy could interrupt, Max added, 'I'm going to take Ricardito into the kitchen for a cookie and some water. I promised him.'

Nancy paused, then nodded her approval. But Max was already gone. 'Dagger, go in there and see if you can help Max until I get another Child Protective Services rep down here. If there are even any more on call tonight,' she sighed.

Dagger went into the kitchen. Max was seated at the table with the little boy on a chair next to her. He was so small that he didn't reach the tabletop, so the paper plate of cookies was on his lap and he clutched one in each fist. Max was talking to him in Spanish.

'I . . . uh, I thought I'd help,' Dagger offered.

'I don't think so,' she replied.

He plopped down onto a chair and reached for a cookie, but he was so tall that his knees crashed against the table and started it rocking. He grabbed for the cup of water just in time. 'Whoa! ' he said. The kid was watching him and smiling. He thought Dagger was funny! 'What's so funny, little man? Huh?' Dagger teased the kid.

Ricardito giggled, pointing to the cup. '*Agua.*'

'He wants water,' Max explained, as if she were talking to an idiot.

'I know that!'

Max reached out her hand. 'Give it to me. I'll give him some.'

'I can get it,' Dagger responded testily.

Max was silent.

Dagger reached over and helped the little boy to sip from the cup. He could feel Max watching him, judging him.

Ricardito gulped and said, 'Ma!'

'Huh? Do I look like your ma to you?' Dagger asked, making a funny face at the kid.

Ricardito laughed. So did Max. 'He said *mas*. He wants more, you goon.'

'Oh, why didn't he say so?' Dagger gave the kid more water. He glanced at Max. Max was looking at him intently, her face unguarded for once. He wanted to forget that they were broken up and mad at each other. He wanted to start again where they had left off before she had gotten stabbed. He wanted to reach over and kiss her, but the little boy was tugging on his sleeve for more water, and then the moment was gone. Max was no longer looking at him but at the floor.

'What happened to his dad?' Dagger asked.

'He doesn't have one. He skipped out.'

Dagger's stomach lurched. Boy, he sure knew how that felt. His dad had disappeared when he wasn't much older than this little guy. He suddenly felt bad for the kid. It was tough to go through life without a mom or a dad. He could totally relate. He looked at the kid and offered him another sip of water.

'Listen,' Max said. 'I know you don't exactly feel like doing me any favors, but I want to go see what's going on with his mom. Can you watch him for a while?'

Dagger stared at her face until she looked straight back at him. 'You want me to stay with the kid?'

'Yeah.

'How about we make a deal? I stay with the kid, you promise to give me ten minutes tonight.'

Max stared at him like he was totally taking advantage of her. 'Forget it,' she said. 'I knew you'd never think of anyone except yourself—'

'Hey!' he interrupted her. 'I *am* thinking of someone else. We have to talk. If this is the only way to get you to do it, then you're stuck, aren't you?'

'Oh, like all of a sudden, now you want to talk to me? Seems you were just fine talking to that other girl, Kyra What's-her-name. What's there to talk about?' Max threw back at him.

Dagger took a deep breath. 'Let's keep her out of it. I just want to clear things up, either way.' No, that was *not* what he meant. 'I mean, I want to talk about us, Max. Come on, give me a break. You know what I mean!'

'No, as a matter of fact, I don't,' she said. She absently handed Ricardito another cookie. Since his hands were full already, he simply dropped one gooey half-eaten one onto his lap and took the new one.

Max was not about to give him an inch, and Dagger knew it. 'Listen, I just want to talk about what's happening with you and me. Okay?'

Max glared at him. 'What's to talk about? We're broken up, remember?'

Time for last resort measures. 'Please?' he offered.

Her face softened. After a few torture-filled moments, she relented. 'Fine. But not till I get back.' She hugged the messy little boy and spoke a few words to him in Spanish.

Dagger watched her leave. Then he looked at the seat in front of him. There he was, alone with the kid. And the kid looked like he wanted something from him. Great! What had he gotten himself into?

'What's up, kid?' he asked.

Ricardito tried to get off the chair, but his hands were full. 'You want to get down?' Dagger asked. 'Then you've got to give me those cookies.' He reached over to pry the cookies out of the kid's hands, but he started to whimper. 'Never mind! Just kidding!' Dagger said, smiling a huge smile.

Ricardito looked pacified, but he still wanted down. Dagger lifted him down but the kid reached his arms up. 'You want me to hold you?' Ricardito grunted. Dagger lifted the kid up. He was surprisingly light. Ricardito pointed to the door. 'All right, kid, let's you and me go on a tour.'

Ricardito smiled and promptly put both his wet, grubby, cookie-filled hands on Dagger's volunteer shirt. 'Oh, mannnn—' Dagger said. 'Look at me! First you think I'm your ma and then you think I'm your napkin!' Ricardito giggled.

Dagger shifted the small child into his right arm and headed out into the ER. As he walked past Nancy's desk, she lifted her eyebrows at him in surprise. 'Uh, we're just going on a little tour.'

'Go figure.' Nancy shook her head with a grin. 'You get back soon, huh? Mrs Conner should be done in a bit.'

'Yes, ma'am!' Dagger saluted. Ricardito's eyes were on his face, watching his every move. 'What? You want to see the elevators? I thought so!' Dagger sauntered over to the elevators and let Ricardito push the button going down. As he waited, a nurse came up to him.

'That your boy?' she asked. 'He's darling!'

Dagger was taken aback. He looked at the kid and realized that they did indeed look alike. Both had light brown skin and dark eyes. The nurse did not wait for his reply.

'What's your name, cutie?' she said.

'Dagger,' he replied.

Her eyes scanned his ID tag and she grinned. 'Not you. Your son.'

Dagger felt too humiliated to correct her. 'Oh, uh, Ricky.'

'What a sweet baby!' she declared, tickling the boy in the ribs and getting a chuckle for her efforts. 'Well, see you!'

While Dagger waited, two more women also stopped by to say hello to the toddler in the tall volunteer's arms. Although his height made him stand out in a crowd, Dagger had never gotten this much attention before. He'd heard that getting a puppy was a sure way to meet girls, but he'd had no idea that kids were such girl magnets. This was kind of cool. Maybe there was something to that lecture Mr Childs had given him about the importance of family when he had balked at going to church at six in the morning with Gran Tootie last week.

The elevator opened and Dagger said to the boy, 'Say bye-bye!'

Thankfully, Ricardito understood and waved. The women waved back and smiled up at Dagger. Inside the elevator, Dagger held on to Ricky and felt the small boy relax in his arms. So this was what it felt like to have someone belong to you. You were totally responsible. Dagger wondered how this kid was supposed to learn about life without a dad. Then it occurred to him that Ricardito might be all alone soon, without his mother, either. If she had AIDS, she was going to die! What would happen to the kid?

Dagger remembered that Max had said that Teresa had no other family. But Nancy had mentioned that Teresa had a brother. Well, then the brother would take the boy, right? Dagger made a mental note to ask Max when she got back.

As he passed the cafeteria, he explained to the boy what it was. Then he did the same with the blood lab. When he reached the doors to the morgue, he paused. He didn't want to lie, but he didn't have to tell the whole truth, now did he? 'And this is where the refrigerators are . . .' Dagger walked around for twenty minutes, the boy in his arms listening to his every word. Dagger didn't even know if he understood or not, but he had a feeling it probably didn't matter. The kid just needed someone to care about him in this big scary place that had swallowed up his mother and left him in the hands of strangers.

Dagger shifted the boy in his arms and was surprised to feel Ricardito clutch onto him, even going so far as to drop his last cookie. 'I won't let you go,' Dagger said reassuringly to the boy. 'Don't you worry.'

Just then the elevator doors opened onto the ER floor and Sara stepped in. Kyle was right behind her pushing an empty supply cart. Great! How was he going to explain this one to the other volunteers? His image would be totally shattered.

Sara grinned. 'Since when did you get a heart, Dagger?'

Dagger smirked at her. 'Since when did you care?'

'Nice kid there, Dagger. Been keeping busy, huh?' Kyle joked.

'Real funny,' Dagger said, and moved out of the elevator as quickly as he could. Where was Max anyway?

Just before the elevator doors closed behind him, he heard Sara murmur, 'How sweet!' Kyle's laughter was cut off.

Dagger walked up to Nancy's desk. 'Where's Max?'

'She was looking for you a while ago. I think she went down to the cafeteria to find you.'

'Oh.' Dagger sighed. 'Well if she comes back up here, tell her I went down there to find her.'

'He seems to have taken a liking to you, Dagger,' Nancy said, commenting on Ricardito's little fists, which were holding on to the fabric of Dagger's shirt like he would never let go.

'Yeah, it's my charm,' Dagger kidded. 'Women and children fall for it all the time.'

Nancy smiled and Dagger made a high sign. To Dagger's surprise, Ricardito tried to imitate him. 'Don't you go corrupting that poor child,' Nancy said.

Dagger knew she was just kidding, but he felt slightly insulted. Didn't anyone trust him to do what was right anymore? He made his way back down to the cafeteria. Max was just getting a soda.

'Where have you been?' Max said accusingly, reaching her arms out for the child. But Ricky grabbed onto Dagger. Both of them were surprised. 'He likes you!' She was clearly astonished.

'Well, why not?' Dagger shot back. 'Only you and

Sara think I'm the boogeyman lately. This kid knows who's cool.'

Max was silent. She sat down and so did Dagger, placing Ricky on his long legs and bouncing him up and down, much to the child's delight.

'What happened to his mom?' Dagger asked.

Max shook her head. 'It doesn't look good. She's had pneumonia for a few weeks and she's already down to about seventy pounds. I asked Dr Kopelow what she thought, and she told me that Teresa probably didn't have long to live.'

'What about the kid?' asked Dagger.

'He's going to have to go to a foster home,' Max replied.

'Why? Doesn't Teresa have a brother?'

'Yeah, but he's got a wife who won't let him take the boy. They all hate Teresa. They think she's bad because her husband ran away or something.'

Dagger was incredulous. 'So they're just going to let the state take him? What a heck of a way to let the kid spend Christmas! What kind of screwed-up family is that?' What was wrong with people? Didn't they know that kids could be harmed for life by being abandoned like that?

'I don't know.' Max looked defeated. 'I swear, I wish I could take him.'

'Yeah . . .' Dagger looked at the kid and smiled. 'He's pretty cool.'

Max stared at him, a surprised expression on her face.

'For a rugrat,' Dagger added hastily. 'Isn't there any organization that takes kids that are – whatcha callit – orphaned from parents with AIDS?'

'No. Not that I know of. And I remember Teresa telling me that she had looked and looked, but there was nothing set up to deal with the kids. Only the parents. And even that was just for food and clothing. Sometimes shelter. It's like they've forgotten all about the kids.'

Dagger felt bad for the boy. Then he recalled a poster by the Pediatric Care Unit. 'Maybe they could find a Big Brother for him or something like that,' he said.

'Maybe.' Max petted Ricky's arm. Her arm brushed Dagger's.

'Hey, Max,' Dagger said, his heart beating a million miles a minute. 'I miss you.'

Max looked up at him. They locked eyes for several seconds. 'Yeah, I miss you, too. But I swear, you make it so hard for me. You just don't know how to act sometimes.'

'Max, I didn't do anything bad! Remember? I never wanted you to be hurt!'

Max gave him a withering look. 'That's not what I'm talking about! You never understood the pressure I was under because school didn't mean as much to you! Didn't I try to spend time with you? It's not like I didn't give you attention!' Max's eyes were filled with tears and Dagger felt like crud.

'You did, you did,' he said, at a loss. He knew that she had let school suffer and had given up sleep just to spend time with him. 'But we still didn't see much of each other.'

'And how could you ask that girl to come here right in front of me? That was totally low!' Max was referring to Kyra. 'Were you trying to get back at me?'

'I didn't ask her! She came by herself! I swear, Max!'

'Yeah, right!'

'No, really!'

Then why did she think it was okay? Didn't you tell her you had an ex-girlfriend here who just might be upset?' Max insisted. She was not about to let this one go. Dagger had not realized she was so jealous.

'I told you that I didn't ask her to come here!'

'Does she even know about me?'

'It was pretty clear to me,' Dagger replied, 'that we were quits. But I still am not responsible for her coming here. I haven't even had time to return her calls, I'm

142

so busy!' He was breathing hard. 'Man! I hate this! Why are we fighting right now?'

Max nodded. 'No kidding. We fought like this all the time.'

'But that doesn't mean we can't work it out!' Dagger whispered fiercely.

'I don't know, Dagger,' said Max quietly. 'It got so serious so fast. I have school to worry about and tests and college . . .' She paused. 'I just don't know if we're going in the same direction. You know?'

'Just because I'm not going to college next year?' he demanded. 'Since when were you so uppity? I thought you were different.'

'It's not just that! I don't mind that you're not going. I just wish you were going to do *something*. I feel like every time I had to study you felt left out – disappointed in me, or something. Like hanging out is what I should be doing all the time. I don't want to spend my whole life hanging out, Dagger!'

'Neither do I!' Dagger shot back. 'Why do you think I'm working so hard now? I'm even getting tutored!'

Max glared at him. 'I'm glad you're working hard. But then what? Are you going to work with Mr Childs for the rest of your life? I want more. I'm getting out of here!'

'Well, right now it's hard enough for me to just hold it all together with my job, Gran Tootie, and this stupid volunteer gig!' Dagger pointed out. 'And I'm sorry if I don't have plans for the next fifty years! I thought that was cool with you.'

'I guess it's not anymore,' Max admitted.

In the heat of their whispered argument, both of them had practically forgotten about the boy. Dagger felt him heavy on his chest. 'What's he doing?' he asked Max.

'He's asleep.' She looked up at him. 'Can't we just declare a truce for now? We can talk next week.'

Dagger wanted more than that – much more. But he could tell that Max was not budging. He nodded and put out a hand. They shook.

'Hey, lovebirds!' Kyle's voice sang across the cafeteria.

Max and Dagger looked up. Dagger was annoyed.

Kyle approached them. 'You make a fine family,' he joked, punching Dagger lightly in the arm. Dagger felt it like a punch to the belly. Leave it to Kyle to say the right thing at the right time – as usual.

Ricardito's eyes fluttered open, then shut again. Dagger shot Kyle a look. 'Watch it! Can't you see he's asleep?' he whispered.

Kyle put his hands up. 'Sorry, papa. Listen, Mrs

Conner's looking for you two. She's got to write up the paperwork on the kid. There's a woman here to take him.'

Max and Dagger exchanged glances. Dagger rose, careful not to wake the child.

Max reached out. 'I'll take him now if you want.'

Dagger paused. Even though Kyle was watching, he didn't feel like letting go of Ricky. Not just yet. He felt like he was betraying the kid somehow. The emotion surprised him. 'Nah, he's asleep,' Dagger replied. 'I'll go up with you.'

Max looked up at him. By her expression, he couldn't tell if she was more upset about the kid or about their relationship.

He didn't know which it was for him, either.

13

The girl's name was Annie. She was sixteen years old, five foot ten, and she weighed ninety-two pounds. Sara knew that she was anorexic, and she knew what the future held for Annie if she didn't start dealing with her eating disorder soon. She would die. She would literally starve herself to death.

Sara had gotten enough information from her to fill out her chart. She was sitting in a cubicle, and Annie was on a gurney, hooked up to an IV which was feeding her liquid food through a tube. Sara had spoken to all sorts of troubled kids when she worked on a crisis hotline, and she had learned about anorexia in her training. That was one of the subjects Ms Dominguez had spent the most time talking about when Sara was being interviewed for the volunteer position at CMH. Sara knew that Ms Dominguez had been a nurse for many years before becoming the volunteer coordinator, and she had specialized in nutrition and eating disorders.

Sara had known girls at her own school who seemed to have eating disorders, but she had never seen anyone who looked as bad as Annie. She sat quietly by the bed while she waited for Ms Dominguez to come in. There were no doctors around to take Annie's history before they moved her into the psych ward, so Ms Dominguez was going to do it. She had told Sara she could sit in since Sara had mentioned a few weeks earlier that she might be interested in psychiatry. Finally, Ms Dominguez pushed aside the curtain to the cubicle and sat down in a chair that put her directly in Annie's frame of vision. Annie just blinked and stared straight through her.

Ms Dominguez picked up the chart, scanned it, and then spoke gently. 'So how did you end up here tonight?' Sara knew that in order to get Annie to deal with her problem, Ms Dominguez first had to get her to acknowledge that she had one.

Annie's eyes stared at the ceiling. 'Like I said, I'm a dancer. I was practicing for a ballet recital at my studio and I guess I just passed out. My friend drove me here.'

'Where is your friend now?' Ms Dominguez asked softly.

'She left. She had to go back. Our teacher is really strict. If we miss practice, we can lose our spot in the recital. There are three other girls who are dying to get the lead. It's very competitive.'

'Do you know why you passed out?'

'I . . . I must just be tired or something,' Annie replied.

'When was the last time you had something to eat?'

'You sound just like my mom!' Annie said scornfully. 'I always eat. I just don't eat a lot, that's all. I can't get fatter than I already am.'

'Do you think ninety-two pounds is fat?'

'Tiffany, another girl in my class, weighs less than me! And she's almost my height!'

'Annie, I know you don't believe me, but you're not fat,' Ms Dominguez replied. 'You have a disease. It's called *anorexia nervosa*. It makes you think you're fat—'

Annie interrupted her. 'You just don't understand! I eat! I do! And I used to be totally fat! I weighed practically one hundred and forty pounds last year! I almost got kicked out of ballet class! My teacher gave me this summer to shape up and I did!'

'Do you throw up after you eat?' Ms Dominguez asked her quietly.

Sara had heard stories about girls totally obsessed with food and weight. She wished she could strangle the sadistic ballet teacher who was encouraging these girls to lose so much weight that they were getting sick.

Annie looked angry. 'Would you just leave me alone?'

'If you throw up after you eat, there's a name for that. It's called *bulimia*. People with bulimia usually binge on food and gorge themselves. Then they feel so bad that they throw it all up afterward. If you do it enough, it gets to the point where you can't control it.' Ms Dominguez paused, touching Annie's free arm. 'You can die, Annie. Is it worth it?' Sara had never seen Ms Dominguez so gentle before.

Annie was quiet. Tears started to run down the sides of her face.

Ms Dominguez started to talk. 'I know how hard it is. I was a big girl, too, when I was your age. I felt awkward and out of place. I'd look in magazines and on TV and see all those pictures of models and actresses who are so slender. You are so sure everyone loves them and thinks they're so beautiful that *you* think you should look like them so people will love and admire you. So you start to diet. And after a while, your friends tell you how great you're looking. And you lose more weight. And you start feeling on top of the world. In control. Only sometimes you get so hungry that you can't help eating. So you throw up if you lose control and overeat. This goes on until it takes over. You can't stop yourself. You hate food. And you hate yourself even more. Pretty soon you end up in the hospital. And if you don't do something, Annie, you might die.'

The girl was silent. She turned her face to the wall.

Sara was shocked. Ms Dominguez never shared anything about her life with the volunteers. It was weird to hear her revealing personal information.

'Annie, I'm going to go call your parents. Someone has to be here with you. But you should be prepared to discuss this with them because the doctor will.' Ms Dominguez stood up, her heels clicking on the parquet. Sara looked at the volunteer coordinator like she was crazy to leave this poor girl here all alone, but she got ready to leave the cubicle anyway.

'They won't listen to you. My parents don't even care about me,' came the strangled little voice. 'They got divorced last year and my dad took my brother and my mom got me. We hate both of them, and they hate us. But we have no choice, 'cause we're just kids.'

Ms Dominguez gave Sara a significant look and sat down again.

'Annie, I'm sure your parents are just confused. Grown-ups don't always know what to do. They don't always do the right thing, either. But you can't starve yourself to death just to punish them.'

'How would you know about it?' Annie demanded sullenly.

'Because my parents didn't stay together. And they didn't act very nicely when they broke up. I wanted them to suffer as much as you want your parents to. I do understand, believe me,' Ms Dominguez said. 'But it's not worth it. Talking to them is. Talking to *anybody* is. But dying isn't.'

'I've been to a shrink! She was an idiot! She wanted to put me on drugs! And my parents agreed with her! But I said no way!'

'Well, maybe you didn't get the right therapist. That doesn't mean you should give up. I bet you could get over this – if you wanted to.'

Annie turned to look at Ms Dominguez. Then her eyes alighted on Sara and traveled up and down Sara's body. 'How do you keep skinny?' Annie asked.

Sara pondered. If she told Annie that she was born that way, it wouldn't help. But if she lied, Annie would be able to tell. 'I eat sensibly and I exercise. I don't deprive myself. And when I go overboard, I don't beat myself up,' she admitted.

Ms Dominguez smiled at Sara.

Annie stared at the tube going into the needle in her arm. 'I guess I understand what you're saying.'

Sara slipped out of the cubicle and leaned up against the wall to get her bearings. When she started volunteering, she used to think she wanted to be a surgeon. But as time went on, she found that it was the people who fascinated her more than their physical bodies. All of their stories were unique. All of them were made up differently. Dealing with all the differences was a challenge that really got her going. Lately, she had been leaning more toward psychiatry. She knew that she would have to go to med school just like any other doctor, but instead of working on the body alone, she would be focusing on the mind and the way the brain and body interacted in a person's psychological makeup. She felt she had a knack for talking to people – even if it was the hardest thing she'd ever done. Ms Dominguez had even noticed it.

Sara went back to the admitting desk. 'Why don't you go find Kyle?' Nancy said. 'We've got two ambulances coming in. A Rollerblading accident and a teenage overdose.'

'Right away,' Sara said. 'Any idea where I might find him?'

Nancy pointed to the supply closet.

'Still?' Sara asked, surprised.

Nancy laughed. 'Ms Dominguez has him on restocking duty except when he's really needed. He'll be busy all night. But this is more important for the moment.'

Sara giggled. 'He's been missing all the action!' She set off toward the supply closet. Just as she went to pull open the door, it pushed toward her from the other side and smacked her in the face. Sara fell back and landed on her rump.

'Hey!' Kyle pushed open the door. 'What—?'

Sara felt her nose. It was wet. She looked at her hands. They were covered in blood!

'Oh, I'm sorry!' Kyle was on his knees. 'Sara!'

Sara looked up at him mournfully. 'By doze!' she said through her hands.

'Here!' He handed her a towel from the stacked cart. 'Put this on it. Can you pinch it?'

Nancy rushed over. 'Move your hands away!' she ordered Sara. She poked and prodded until Sara thought she might faint. ' It's not broken. Kyle, take her into the lounge and put ice on this. I don't want you to move for thirty minutes. It'll stop bleeding soon enough.'

'But what about the ambulances?' Sara said. 'If it's not broken—'

Nancy interrupted her, an incredulous look on her face. 'It's not you I'm worried about! You think the patients want a volunteer bleeding all over them?'

Sara laughed through her pain at the image. Kyle looked relieved. 'I'm so sorry! Here, let's go into the lounge. Keep your head up. I'll lead you.'

Sara allowed Kyle to take her into the lounge. They passed Dagger and Max on the way. 'What happened?' Max cried.

'Nothing. Not broken. Just a bump,' Sara said, her voice muffled through the towel.

'Are you guys free or is this coffee-break time?' Nancy called out to Max and Dagger. 'I got two coming in. You want to get your butts out to the bay?'

'I'll come in to see you later,' Max whispered to Sara.

Sara grunted and let Kyle lead her into the lounge. He helped her lie down on the sofa and then she heard him taking ice cubes out of the tray in the freezer.

'You want an ice pack or ice cubes?'

'Cubes,' she said.

'Coming right up.' She heard him run the water and then remove the bloody towel. He held up a cold, wet towel wrapped around ice. 'Just lean back,' Kyle said.

Sara looked sideways at him. He looked so darned sorry that she started to giggle again. 'Gosh, Kyle, it's not the end of the world.'

'I know,' he said. 'I just' – he paused – 'I just can't believe I hurt you.'

He was really going overboard! What was this all about? 'Well, if it had to happen anywhere, I guess this is the place,' she joked. 'Besides, if you want to know the truth, my butt hurts more than my nose!'

'You want some ice for it?' Kyle offered without thinking.

Sara grinned. 'Kyle!'

He looked at her and then she saw something amazing: Kyle Cullen blushed from the roots of his hair all the way down his neck.

Just then Max came into the lounge. 'Kyle, can you take over for me? Dagger's in Trauma One with the guy who was brought in from that skating accident. The second ambulance with the overdose is going into Trauma Room Two. It's not here yet. Please?'

Kyle jumped up. Sara knew he had been bored out of his gourd all night long doing supply duty. 'Are you going to be okay?' he asked her.

'Go. I'll survive. Really!' she insisted.

The two girls watched him race out of the lounge.

'So, you two looked kind of cozy there,' Max said wryly.

'Get out of here!' Sara replied. 'He was just feeling bad because he was the one who did it, that's all.'

'Whatever you say.'

Sara noticed that Max sounded down. 'What's wrong?'

Max pursed her mouth.

'Bad night?' Sara commented.

'Understatement of the year,' Max sighed. 'First, they're going to take this tiny boy away to a foster home because his mother's about to die of AIDS. Then Dagger and I got into it. I swear, college is probably a cinch compared to this gig!'

'What happened?' Sara sat up.

Max looked alarmed. 'Shouldn't you be lying down?'

'Nah, I think it's stopped. Is it dripping?' Sara tilted up her head.

'No, all clear. But just keep that ice on it anyway.'

'Are you going to tell me?'

'Yes!' Max waited for Sara to get adjusted, then spoke. 'He tried to explain everything. It's both our faults . . .'

'Maybe he just didn't know what he wanted yet,' Sara said, surprised at herself for defending Dagger on this point.

Max smiled sadly. 'Thanks, Sara. That's true, especially since I know you weren't really excited about him being my boyfriend. But *he's not* in the past tense.'

'What do you mean?'

'I mean that I still care. A lot,' Max admitted.

Sara thought for a moment. 'Well, do you think you guys can work it out? Do you think you can learn to trust each other?'

Max shrugged. 'I don't know. It seems like no matter how hard I try, I can't do the work for both of us. He has to try, too. I hate feeling like I'm always pushing.'

'Where is it you want to go so badly?' Sara asked.

'I don't know!' Max said strongly. 'Now that he has that construction job and Mr Childs is tutoring him for the equivalency exam, I feel a little better. I know he won't be another homeboy hanging out on the streets.' She paused. 'I'm just scared, that's all. All this week in bed, I kept thinking that I could be dead because of who I was hanging out with. No other reason than that. It was terrible!'

'You know, Max, it really sounds like you want to give Dagger another chance,' Sara said.

'We'll see. Anyway, forget this. I'm just going to hang back and see how things go. No commitment either way,' Max said, indicating that the conversation about her and Dagger was closed. 'So, we've talked enough about my problems. What about yours?'

'Hmmm?'

'Your mom. Remember her?'

'What about her?' Sara replied.

Max gave Sara a look. 'What are you going to do?'

Sara was silent as she pulled the wet towel off her face. Her nose had stopped bleeding and felt fine. She sat up. 'Actually, I'm pretty sure I am going to call her after all. I'm just not sure what to say, you know?'

Max nodded. 'Well, what about just asking her to meet you sometime? That way you can stop obsessing about it!'

'Oh, right, then all I'll obsess about is what I'm going to say when we do meet!'

'What if you limit the time you meet? Like set it up so you can only talk for a few minutes. That way you get to see her, check her out, and see if she's really changed or if she's making it all up.'

Sara was stunned. 'How did you know I was thinking about that?'

'You think I haven't been paying attention all this time we've been friends?' Max replied with a giggle. 'I know how your mind works – because it works a lot like mine!'

Sara laughed. Then she got serious. 'How about I ask her to meet me here next week?'

'Here at CMH?' asked Max.

'Why not? I can ask her to meet me during a break, like at the end of the night or something. 'That way it can't last longer than I want it to.'

'And if you do it on your last break, I can be here for you. And you won't have to work more than a few hours afterward if it goes really bad,' Max finished.

Sara nodded. 'Perfect! Maybe I'll go call her right now. Will you cover for me?'

Max jumped up. 'Of course! I'll tell Nancy you went to wash up your face in the locker room. You can call from the phones down there.'

Sara's heart began to pound. 'Max?'

Max turned at the door, took one look at her, and came over to her. 'Don't worry,' she said, 'you'll be really glad you did. Trust me. And if it goes badly, at least you'll know you tried.'

Sara smiled. Max was right. She hugged her friend and slipped out toward the locker room. On the way down, all she could think of was that she had been looking forward to this moment for six years – and dreading it also.

In the locker room, she removed the number from her backpack. It was a Tucson number. Sara fished around in her change purse but could only find twenty-six cents. Darn! What about using her credit card? No, her dad would kill her if he found out. Sara couldn't believe her misfortune. She had been thinking about this forever and now that she had finally found the courage, she couldn't do it! Then she recalled that her mother had told her to call collect.

Here goes.

She punched in the ten digits. The operator came on the line.

'Yes?' the operator prompted her impatiently.

'Uh, collect call from Sara Greenberg.'

'Hold the line, please.'

Sara's heart thumped loudly and her tongue was plastered to the roof of her mouth. Her mind was racing: *What is taking so long? What if it's the wrong number? What if she moved in the last three weeks? What if she has decided she doesn't want to talk to me after all? What if—?*

'Hello? Sara? Hello?'

It was her mother. She sounded sober, all right – if Sara was remembering correctly, that is. She tried to picture her mother the last time she had seen her: She had been standing at the front door in her bathrobe, a cigarette in one hand and a martini glass in the other. She had shattered Sara's life when she had yelled at her never to come back, to go to her father's where she belonged. Sara had sat on the lawn in tears, willing the front door to unlock. All her belongings were inside, including her keys. There was no way to get back inside. Finally, as the sun slipped beneath the horizon,

Sara had made her way over to a neighbor's house and called her father. That had been over six years ago. But this woman didn't sound incoherent and drunk. She sounded – almost – normal. For the first time in a long time, Sara was speechless.

'Sara? Honey? I'm so glad you called! Are you there?'

'I'm here.' Sara suddenly forgot why she called. But then Max's words came tumbling through her brain again: '*What if you limit the time you meet? Like set it up so you can only talk for a few minutes. That way you get to see her, check her out, and see if she's really changed or if she's making it all up.*' Sara tried again. 'I thought it might be a good idea if we set up a meeting. A short one. For a few minutes. If it works out, then we can talk more later.' Sara couldn't believe how grown-up her voice sounded – even to herself!

Her mother didn't even hesitate. 'I would love that. You just tell me when and where and I'll be there.'

14

Max ran out of the locker room and headed down the hall to Trauma Room Two. She knew Kyle was probably happy where he was, but she didn't want to leave him working in the crash room for long. Ms Dominguez had to be pretty mad at Kyle to assign him to supply duty, and Max didn't want to make it worse. There was enough trouble around without adding to it.

Max pulled open the door of the Trauma Room. Connie and a doctor Max had never seen before were bending over a skinny teenage girl with an oxygen mask over her face.

'How's her pulse?' the doctor demanded.

'Still erratic,' Connie replied.

'She must have taken something besides heroin or the naloxone would have taken care of it,' the doctor said briskly.

'How quickly is the blood work on her going to come back?'

'They said ten minutes,' Kyle piped up eagerly.

'Then we better pump her stomach,' the doctor declared. 'She may have taken some kind of barbiturate in addition to the heroin. That might be what's inhibiting her respiration.'

Connie nodded and got to work, getting the necessary equipment in place. Meanwhile Max moved forward, signaling Kyle with her eyes that it was time for him to go back to supply duty. Kyle looked so crestfallen that Max almost felt sorry for him. It was incredible how much he loved being on the scene of any medical procedure, no matter how gory, Max thought, grinning slightly to herself. Then she stopped smiling.

The girl on the gurney looked like she was in bad shape. The insides of her skeletally thin arms were covered with bruises and scabs. Track marks. Her bones jutted out even through her dirty, baggy clothes. The girl looked like she hadn't been living at home for a long time. *She's probably been on the street for months*, Max reflected soberly. This girl couldn't be much older than she was, but she already looked worn out, used up – like a crumpled paper cup or a dented old soda can. Even if the girl made it this time, she didn't look like she'd be around to see her old age. If she was shooting up, there was a good chance she already had some infection like hepatitis or AIDS.

Max was saddened. Thinking about AIDS made her think about Teresa again. She wondered how Teresa was doing. Probably not well. When the EMS technicians carried Teresa out of the ambulance, Max had hardly recognized her. Teresa had gotten so thin that she looked like a walking skeleton – a shadow.

Max watched intently as the doctor put a tube down the girl's throat and started water flowing through it to clear out the girl's stomach. 'Bring me another container of water,' Connie ordered, pointing at the containers of filtered water in the corner.

Max went to get the water. If Teresa died, Ricardito would go to a foster home for sure. And there was no way Teresa wasn't going to die – if not tonight, then soon.

'Well, that should take care of whatever's in there,' the doctor said five minutes later. 'Now we'll just have to monitor her and see how she does.'

Connie nodded. Then she turned to Max. 'Why don't you go down to the lab and see if they've finished her blood work yet?' she suggested.

'Sure,' Max said. She sped out of the room. She was glad to get out of there. She was secretly hoping that she might come across Ricardito in the hall somewhere. Mrs Conner had filled out some paperwork for him and told Max that a woman had come to take him. *But what woman?* Max wondered. *And where's she going to take Ricardito?* She couldn't stand to think that Ricardito would just be taken away somewhere without ever seeing his mother or anyone he knew again.

Max went up to the lab window. The blood work on the overdose was finished. Max tucked it under her arm and headed back. There was no sign of Ricardito anywhere.

Fighting an overwhelming feeling of disappointment, Max strode back into the Trauma Room. She gave the blood results on the patient to Connie, who handed the yellow paper to the doctor without a word. 'I was afraid of that,' the doctor murmured. 'What a shame. A girl this young, HIV-positive.'

HIV-positive? Max thought bleakly.

'Well, Max, I think we're about done here for now,' Connie said. 'Why don't you go see if Nancy needs help?'

'Sure thing,' Max said.

She trudged out of the room, slowly this time. In the hall, she saw Dagger. A blush spread over her cheeks. After their latest argument, Dagger probably wouldn't be all that happy to see her. 'Hey,' she said awkwardly.

'Hey,' Dagger said.

'Um, I know this sounds dumb, but have you seen Ricardito anywhere?'

'No,' Dagger replied abruptly. 'I guess he was taken away.'

'You haven't heard anything about Teresa?'

'No.' Dagger shook his head.

'Well, thanks—' Max started to say when she looked up and saw Ricardito. He was being carried down the hall by Teresa's brother, Hector. Max could hardly believe it. Hector was holding the little boy tightly, and a woman who must have been his wife was right behind him. The woman was dabbing a handkerchief at her red, swollen eyes. As Max watched, Hector said something to her, and she turned and headed toward the elevators. Then he sat down heavily in a chair by the front lobby. Still holding Ricardito close to his chest, he began to talk to the boy in Spanish.

Max could hear the rhythm of the words, but she wasn't close enough to hear what Hector was saying. Slowly she inched forward, not wanting to intrude but desperate to know what was going on.

Hector looked up and saw her coming toward him. He nodded stiffly. But Ricardito smiled and reached out for Max with his tiny hands. As Ricardito scrambled up into her arms, she looked over at Hector. Now that she was close, she could see that he'd been crying.

'How's Teresa doing?' she asked quietly in Spanish.

Hector shook his head. 'She died half an hour ago,' he replied, also in Spanish. 'Even with all those doctors working on her, she just couldn't make it. She asked them to take all the machines off her. She said she'd been fighting a long time and she just didn't have the strength to fight anymore. She was a good fighter, Teresa, but—' Hector broke off for a second. 'When they took the machines off,' he went on hoarsely, 'her breath rattled for a minute. Then it just stopped. She looked so small when it was over. Like she was a kid again. Little Teresa.'

'I'm so sorry,' Max whispered. She felt a lump in her throat.

'So am I,' Hector said. 'I'm sorry for many things.' He looked right at Max. 'We decided to keep Ricardito,' he added simply. 'We told that woman, Mrs Conner, that we would adopt him into our family. It's only right. I couldn't let my own nephew go to some stranger's house.'

Hector paused. 'My wife said,' he continued haltingly, 'she said . . . well . . . we were wrong. She was wrong. See, we always thought, you know, you had to be a bad person to get that disease like Teresa did. But after we watched her die, my wife and I, we knew that no one should have to suffer like that. No one. It's a bad disease, but it's got nothing to do with the person.' Hector looked down at his feet.

Max circled her arms tighter around Ricardito. She wondered how much he understood of what was happening, whether he understood that his mother was really gone.

The elevator doors opened. Hector's wife stepped out carrying a cardboard tray with coffee for her and Hector and a carton of milk for Ricardito. She looked at Max.

'Hector told you,' she said softly.

'Yes,' Max nodded.

Hector's wife's eyes filled with tears. 'I never knew I was being so unfair, hating her like that,' she sniffed. Her chin jutted out, and she stared straight at Max. 'Don't worry. We'll take good care of Ricardito,' she said. Then she leaned down toward the little boy. '*Hola*, Ricardito!' she crooned, holding out the carton of milk. Ricardito reached out for her, and she gave the tray to her husband and took the boy out of Max's arms. Lifting a straw from the tray, she began helping Ricardito drink the milk.

Max felt a lump rising in her throat. She swallowed hard to choke it down. 'I'd love to come see Ricardito some time,' she said politely in Spanish. 'And if you ever need a baby-sitter, let me know, okay?'

'Of course,' Hector's wife replied. 'You're welcome to come see Ricardito anytime. Right, Hector?'

Hector looked incredibly sad for a moment. Then he forced himself to smile. 'Right,' he agreed. 'Anytime.'

'Max! Over here!'

Max turned to see Nancy frantically signaling her from the admitting desk. As usual, Nancy had a stack of patient charts in front of her a foot high.

'I'm coming,' Max called. Then she squeezed Ricardito's hand in hers, feeling his small, warm fingers. 'Ricardito, I'll come see you real soon. I promise,' she told him in Spanish.

For a moment, the child's eyes looked into hers. Ricardito's eyes were wide and scared. Then slowly, his small chubby face broke into a smile.

'Bye-bye!' he said.

'Bye!'

Blinking fast, Max turned and quickly rushed off down the hall.

15

Kyle raced out to the ambulance bay and waited for the wagon to arrive. The call had come over the EMS computer three minutes ago. An ambulance was arriving any minute with *another* teenage overdose – a boy this time. It was a bad night for kids and drugs, Kyle thought. CMH handled plenty of drug cases, but two overdoses in less than an hour was a lot, even for them. Since everyone else was busy, Nancy told Kyle he could briefly get off supply duty again to help out.

A few blocks away he heard the sirens shut off. Regulations required that ambulance sirens wind down before reaching CMH. It was better that way both for the neighboring homes and for the patients already at the hospital. Sirens were meant to be alarming.

As he waited, Kyle thought about Sara. He felt really bad about bumping into her before. But the worst was when he had tried to move her bangs out of her face and she had moved away. She really had no interest in him at all. He was totally disappointed. *I guess Josh is still on her mind*, he thought.

The ambulance backed up rapidly into the bay and discharged its occupants. Kyle stepped aside as the stretcher was rushed into the ER.

'Age?'

'Fifteen, sixteen.'

'Substance?'

'Alcohol plus. We just don't know what the plus is.'

'BP low and breathing shallow.'

'He was unconscious for approximately ten minutes before we showed up.'

'Showed up?'

'Nightclub.'

Kyle listened as the EMS guys moved to the back of Trauma Room Two. The doctors transferred the boy onto a hospital gurney. The paperwork was handed over. Kyle strained to hear every word.

The on-call doctor, Dr Martinez, quizzed the resident as they checked the kid over from head to toe.

'Track marks?'

'Negative,' replied the resident.

'You check between the toes?'

The resident looked up, an incredulous look on his face.

'Toes! Toes!' yelled Dr Martinez impatiently. 'It's the best place to hide the needle marks from parents, friends—'

'—and stupid doctors,' confirmed the resident. 'How did you know? Look at this.'

Dr Martinez leaned in and examined what Kyle imagined were the marks. 'There might be more on his stomach. Never know what these kids are mixing. From the look of the tracks, this kid wasn't new to this. He might've added a new ingredient tonight. Let's pump him.'

For the second time that night, a tube was inserted into a patient's mouth and down his throat and the kid's stomach was pumped. 'The benefits will be minimal. Most of it's already been absorbed into the bloodstream,' the doctor announced. 'All we can do now is wait to see if he wakes up. Let's get him on oxygen and pump him up with some counterindicative medication. Then he goes to the ICU where he can be monitored. Twenty-four hour watch.'

Kyle scanned the monitors hooked up to the kid and thought about how stupid drugs were. How could anyone know what their effects could be? One night of supposed fun and you could spend the rest of your life as a vegetable – or worse, you could die. It was pretty scary. Kids died all the time from drug overdoses, yet their friends never seemed to get the message.

Kyle slipped out of the Trauma Room. He glanced at the clock and was surprised to see that it was just about midnight. The other volunteers would be going home now. Sara had been in the lounge half an hour ago, and he supposed she was now getting ready to leave. Max was just finishing up in Admitting. The last he'd seen of Dagger had been when he had slipped him the articles about the girls from last week's newspaper. Even Nancy was packing up for the night, waiting for another nurse to arrive and take over. Kyle was psyched to do his make-up time tonight. Why not? Doctors pulled all-nighters all the time. He could even pretend that he was a doctor and Carrie was his patient by checking up on her in between endlessly restocking, just to get a feel for it. It would be exciting to be the only volunteer on duty in the ER during the graveyard shift.

Nancy introduced Kyle to Regina, the replacement admitting nurse. 'Reg, he's on restock duty when it's quiet, so don't let him charm you out of it.'

'No problem, Nancy,' Regina said. But while her voice was serious, she winked at Kyle. She waited until Nancy had gone and said, 'So how come you're here so late? We never get volunteers on the late shift.

Must have been bad to get you supply closet duty, though.' She chuckled.

Kyle wanted to tell her something that would make him look heroic, but he had a feeling she wouldn't buy it. 'I stayed too long in the operating forum. This girl was brought in last week for a torn aorta. She's up in the sixth-floor ICU. I'd love to see how she's doing tonight. Anyway, I just didn't pay attention to the time and Ms D. nabbed me.'

Regina looked at him. 'I know Nancy and Chelly. They'd never punish someone for caring. I'm sure they have their reasons.'

Kyle felt foolish – and defensive. Why was she so interested? 'Yeah. I guess so. I'll just go get that cart filled up.'

'You do that.' She stood up and seemed to waver slowly. Her face drained of color and she placed a hand on her chest.

Kyle raced to her side. 'Are you okay? What's wrong? Are you all right?' He tried to help her sit back down.

She held on to his arm and plopped into her chair. 'Oh yeah, I'm fine. Thanks. Probably just tired. Had a long day.' She took a sip of water and smiled up at him.

'You sure? You don't look so hot,' Kyle said. 'Not

that I'm a doctor or anything. It's just that—'

'Don't worry about me,' Regina said, interrupting him. 'I'll be fine. Just a little tired, I said. Listen, why don't you go check up on that patient, then come back down and hit those supply closets. You'll probably learn more up there in fifteen minutes than you will down here all night anyway.'

Kyle could not believe how nice she was being. 'Really? Great! I'll come right back.'

He took the elevator up to the Cardiac Care Unit. Carrie was in the east wing ICU. Volunteers were allowed to enter the Intensive Care Units as long as they did not interfere with the doctors and nurses there. ICU patients were monitored twenty-four hours a day with one nurse assigned to a patient. While many ICU patients were simply recovering from the trauma of extensive surgeries like heart bypasses or transplants, some were so critically injured that they would never make it out of there.

Kyle entered the sixth floor ICU, where cardiac care patients were kept. He approached the nurse at the O-shaped desk which afforded a view of all the beds. Each patient was in his or her own small room. All had glass walls so that the patients were clearly visible from many angles. Monitors and screens lined the back walls. The hiss of oxygen and the pumping of machines were the only sounds besides the movement of the staff. It was very quiet compared to the ER

'Hi. I'm looking for a patient named Carrie,' Kyle said. He had learned long ago that it was not necessary to announce that he was a volunteer to the hospital staff since the color of his shirt indicated his position quite clearly.

The nurse looked at him over the top edges of her bifocals. 'You family?'

'No. But I was on when she was first brought in. I was just wondering—' He was interrupted by the screech of a machine. The nurse's eyes darted to the bank of screens in front of her and pressed a button. 'We got an alarm,' she announced to the nurse at her left. 'Call Dr Tytel. It's her patient.'

As if a magic button had been pushed, the staff moved into action. Kyle moved out of the way as he tried to figure out who the patient was. Two surgical residents were hovering over a patient in the room directly behind him.

Dr Tytel came rushing in. 'Is it Carrie?'

The nurse nodded. 'Respiratory distress of some sort.' Dr Tytel whizzed by her into the room. Kyle followed her and stood out of the way as the team encircled her bed.

'She's in ARDS,' declared the ICU nurse assigned

to Carrie. If Kyle remembered correctly, ARDS meant acute respiratory distress syndrome.

'My guess is her lungs got wet. They're probably discharging fluid outside the arteries,' said Dr Tytel. 'Let's get those drugs going!'

Carrie was still unconscious and had been for a week since she was brought in. They injected her with paralyzing drugs so that her body would not demand further oxygen, and pumped her full of narcotics to calm her and to modulate the controls on the ventilator she was hooked up to. Oxygen was forced into her lungs.

Kyle watched for what seemed like an eternity as the residents and nurses worked the controls, fighting the wildly fluctuating up and down of her blood pressure. At one point a resident cried out, 'Her pressure is still falling!'

'Come on, Carrie!' Dr Tytel urged, working over the young woman. 'Don't give up on us now!'

Kyle feared what everyone else there did: that the fight to save her life was lost. They continued to work the ventilator and to feed her more drugs so that she would not fight the ventilator. But it was a delicate balance. Too little of the drug would not sedate her enough, but too much would lower her blood pressure into the danger zone.

Finally, the team managed to stabilize Carrie's respiratory system. Kyle thought that he had witnessed a miracle. He pondered what Ms Dominguez had told him about teamwork and saw, not for the first time, how efficiently the doctors, nurses, and techs at CMH worked in a crisis.

After a while, the team dispersed. Only the ICU nurse in charge of Carrie stayed put next to her bed. Kyle slipped into the room. What he saw made him gasp. Carrie did not look at all like a miracle. Because of the fluids accumulating in her body due to the trauma of her injuries, she was almost twice the size she had been when brought in. Her hands were like catcher's mitts, her tongue was as bloated as a cow's, and her face was so engorged that her eyes were nearly invisible.

The nurse whispered, 'She doesn't look so great, but she's much better than she was a week ago. We just hope she regains consciousness.'

Kyle noticed that Carrie's legs were twitching, and soon they almost appeared to be having their own little seizure. The nurse checked one of the IVs and opened it up to allow more fluid to drip in.

'What's that for?' Kyle asked.

'The pain makes her limbs flail. She ends up dislodging the tubes that keep her alive. These drugs practically paralyze her, but we have to administer them to save her,' the nurse explained.

'Are those staples?' Kyle asked, pointing to the small series of lines across her bloated face.

'Yes, the plastic surgeon closed her injuries. In a few days they'll fit a rod into that fracture on her leg. She's got a long way to go.'

'Do you think she'll make it?' Kyle asked.

The nurse smiled. 'I think so. She's a fighter, this one. I think when she's ready, she'll wake up and tell us all to go to hell!'

'I hope so.' Kyle thanked her and left the ICU. On his way over to the elevator, he heard the loudspeaker. 'Volunteer to ER. Volunteer to ER.'

Kyle started. It was a man's voice. Usually the admitting nurse was the one who called the volunteers. He glanced at his watch. He had been gone for a while! 'Shoot!' he said, and opted for the stairs which were faster than the elevators even at this time of night. What was wrong with him? He was definitely having a problem with this time thing. All he needed was to get reported to Ms Dominguez again. She'd have his head – and kick it down the sidewalk out of CMH for good measure if she found out he had been missing again.

His heart beating wildly, he practically ran into the ER. There, lying behind the desk on the floor, was

Regina, getting CPR from a sweating resident. A tech and an attending physician that Kyle had never seen before were also working on her.

Sam, the security guard, pulled Kyle aside. 'We're short-staffed tonight, kid. Can you handle the charts for a while?' Sam indicated the stack of charts for patients who had yet to be admitted.

'Yeah, sure. What happened to her?' Kyle asked.

'Don't know. She passed out. Stopped breathing,' Sam explained.

'No time to move her. Let's get an IV going!' They watched as a nurse inserted an IV and hooked her up.

'We've got some idioventricular rhythm here!' cried the attending doctor. 'Any pulse yet?'

'No pulse. I need to intubate! Stop CPR!' replied the resident.

Kyle watched. Why were they stopping Regina's CPR if she wasn't breathing?

'We've got a definite rhythm on the monitor. Appears to be idioventricular, perhaps junctional. Regular, at a rate of fifty-four beats per minute.' The resident was tense.

'Maybe EMD,' said the attending physician. 'Try a fluid challenge.' He grabbed a large injection of fluid and put it into the IV tubing, continuing the CPR again.

'Stop CPR! The rhythm is V-fib!'

Kyle watched as the paddles were charged and placed on the nurse's chest. 'Everybody clear!' called out the attending physician. Kyle heard the loud noise signaling the machine was ready; then the body jumped with two hundred joules of electricity.

'Check a pulse.'

'No pulse. Still V-fib. Fire again.'

'Clear!' Again the doctor defibrillated, this time at three hundred.

'Check a pulse.'

'No pulse. Defibrillate at three-sixty. Clear!'

'No pulse. Continue CPR.'

'Epi in. Check a pulse.'

'No pulse.'

'Clear! Fire!'

'Lidocaine. Bolus and drip.'

'Defibrillate at three-eighty. Clear!'

'No pulse. Continue CPR.'

Sweaty and tense, the attending physician tried one thing, then another. The team moved over her like a well-rehearsed swarm of bees. Kyle watched as they tried again and again, but the body was unresponsive. After what seemed like forever, the doctor stood up. 'I'm sorry, everybody. We tried.' He signed a few papers and handed them to one of the nurses, shaking his head sadly. He looked at her one last time and headed back into one of the cubicles.

As two orderlies placed Regina's body on a gurney, one of the techs began to cry. Others stood around awkwardly – no one wanted to leave and no one knew what to say. As an orderly drew a sheet over her, the crowd began to disperse. Kyle overheard one of the doctors contacting Regina's husband – they would want to do an autopsy.

Kyle was shocked. She was dead? The admitting nurse was dead? Since when did staffers die? He moved back as they wheeled her gurney down the hall.

Sam approached Kyle. 'Things like this just don't make sense,' he said glumly. 'She was my friend. Talking to her always made the late shift go by faster. You couldn't say a bad word about her.'

The security phone rang. Sam answered. 'Sure. I'll let them know. Thanks.' He turned back to Kyle. 'We're looking for another AN to take over here,' Sam said. 'Should only be a minute or so. Then I'm off for tonight. Can you handle this?'

Kyle nodded. 'Yeah. I'm fine. I just can't believe it.' He thought about Regina. She had been nice to him for two minutes and now he'd never be able to forget her.

'Listen, kid, it happens sometimes,' Sam said gently.

'They'll find out tomorrow what made her ticker give out. What can I tell you?'

Kyle nodded blankly and watched Sam leave. Out of the corner of his eye, he saw two orderlies wheeling a gurney out of Trauma Room Two toward the elevator. It was the kid who'd been brought in earlier who'd overdosed. Now he was awake – thrashing around and shouting that he wanted them to let him out of there.

Kyle's shoulders slumped. He supposed he should be glad the kid had pulled through okay, but all he could think about was Regina. He went over to where she'd been sitting an hour before and picked up the first chart in the stack at the corner of the admitting desk. He read the chart as he moved out to the waiting area. Regina's handwriting was nearly illegible. All he could make out was *Female. Age 20. Amnesia. See escort, male.*

Kyle scanned the room for anyone looking like a twenty-year-old female with amnesia. There was a middle-aged man over in a corner sitting next to a young woman with a panicked look on her face. Her eyes were darting all over the room. He made his way over to her. The man stood up.

'She can't tell you who she is,' he stated. 'There's something wrong with the little lady.'

'Okay,' Kyle replied, sitting down. 'Can you tell me who she is?'

'Nope. I found her sleepin' right up on my front porch tonight. I invited her in to warm up some, but she was too scared. I finally called my neighbor, a lady, to come over and help. Seems like she doesn't know anything about herself or where she is.' The man looked kind and sounded genuinely concerned to Kyle.

'Is she hurt at all?' asked Kyle.

'Not that I can tell, though it looks like she could use some food and a bath.'

Kyle nodded. 'Do you think you can stay with her until the doctor can see her?'

The man nodded. 'I brought her this far. I reckon I can stay some more.'

Kyle made a few notes on the chart and returned to the admitting desk, where he filed it under the nonurgents. He yawned and looked at the clock. It was three in the morning. Man, was he tired! And he still had three more hours to go! The waiting room was packed and he was in desperate need of some caffeine, but there was no way he could skip out now to the soda machine. What had he been thinking when he decided to do this? Maybe he wasn't cut out to be a doctor after all.

Just deal, man. It was Alec's voice running through his head. Whenever something came up that Kyle found hard to deal with, his brother Alec would offer those words. *Just deal, bro.* Only now Alec was in an institution fighting off depression and it was Kyle's turn to pass on those words of wisdom.

Kyle sighed and grabbed another chart. *Zachary Cohen. Infant, 1 year. Beans up nose.* Great! Kyle went back out to the waiting room where two exhausted-looking parents were holding a baby boy. The child was sleeping peacefully. 'Mr and Mrs Cohen?'

'Yes?' The mother shot up, nearly upsetting the sleeping baby on her husband's shoulder. 'Are you ready for us? Should I wake the baby?'

'No, no. Not yet. I just want to make sure I have all your information here. How is he?' Kyle asked.

'He's fine,' said the husband, patting his anxious wife's arm. 'We can see the peas, but we just couldn't get them out. He's breathing just fine through his mouth.'

'It says *beans* here. Are they peas or beans?' Kyle asked, feeling slightly foolish. Did it matter?

'They're hard peas. The nurse we spoke to kept getting it wrong,' the wife answered rapidly. 'I *told* you, honey, that she'd get it wrong. It's *peas*. What if it goes into his brain? When can we see a doctor?

We've been here almost an hour already. That stupid nurse promised us an hour ago . . .'

Kyle wondered what this woman would say if she knew that she was slamming a dead person. 'Why don't I take you into a cubicle to wait?' was all he said. Nancy had always told him that hysterical parents were likely to get the entire waiting room in an uproar, so whenever possible, it was a good idea to take agitated ones into a cubicle, even if it didn't make any difference as to the time they'd have to wait.

'That's more like it!' said the mother. 'Come on, Joe, let's go. Be careful not to joggle the baby!'

Kyle led them into cubicle three and pulled the curtain shut. Three more hours. Had he really been excited to stay on for another shift? Was he nuts?

16

Kyle ran back over to the admitting desk and picked up another chart. *Mr Brian Murray. Age 52. Chest pain. Possible angina.* Another patient with heart trouble! Kyle let out his breath in a long, shuddering sigh. He didn't know if he could deal with that after Regina. But what choice did he have? There was no one else around. He was about to call out Mr Murray's name when a voice behind him said, 'Kyle, I'll take care of this chart. Why don't you take the next one?'

Kyle turned around to see Martha Rodgers standing behind him. The young nurse usually worked the earlier shift – Kyle's regular shift – and she usually worked on the EMS computer, not at the admitting desk.

'Martha,' Kyle gasped in relief. 'How did you get here so fast?'

'I was on call,' Martha replied simply. 'When you're on call and they tell you to show up, you show up in a hurry.'

'I bet.' Kyle noticed Martha's eyelids were pink and swollen. It could be just from lack of sleep, but Kyle had a feeling it was because she'd been crying. 'I guess you heard about Regina,' he stammered awkwardly.

'Yes,' Martha replied. 'She was a good friend of mine.'

'I'm sorry,' Kyle said helplessly. 'I never met her before tonight but I can tell – I mean, she was really, really nice to me, and I know she was a good person.'

'You're right about that,' Martha agreed. Her eyes met Kyle's, and they both looked away.

Kyle picked up the next chart on the pile. He was glad Martha was there – glad he wasn't going to have to do this all alone. But every time he thought about Regina, his chest felt tight. It was bad enough when patients died, but it was a hundred times worse when one of the staff died, Kyle thought, biting his lip. The people who worked together in the hospital were members of a team. They relied on each other so much that when something happened to one of them, it was hard to go on.

'Kyle, are you all right?' Martha prodded him gently.

'Yeah, sure.'

'Then go on and take care of that chart.' Martha gave him a fleeting smile. 'Don't worry,' she added in an undertone. 'We'll make it.'

Kyle just nodded. Then he went into the waiting room and called out the name on the chart. 'Isaac Rostavitch?'

'He's over here,' someone called out loudly. It was an elderly woman with gray hair pulled back into a bun who was sitting next to a white-haired man with a neatly trimmed beard. The man smiled as Kyle walked up. He had a nice face. He looked like a wise old professor.

'Well, Mr Rostavitch, what seems to be the problem?'

'There isn't any problem,' the old man said stoutly. 'I'm perfectly fine. It's just my wife. She likes to make a fuss.'

'Isaac, that's not true,' the woman said anxiously. 'You're sick. I know you are.'

'Sophia, I'm fine.' The old man patted her hand.

'He's not fine,' the woman said to Kyle urgently.

Kyle cleared his throat. 'Well, what seems to be the problem?' he repeated.

Mrs Rostavitch twisted her hands together. 'I don't know how to describe it,' she murmured. 'He sees things, but he doesn't see them. He can't see them!'

'You mean, it's his eyes?' Kyle asked, confused.

'It's not his eyes. It's – look.' Mrs Rostavitch held up the coffee cup she was drinking from. 'Isaac,' she said, turning to her husband, 'what am I holding?'

The old man stared at the cup intently. 'It is a small, cylindrical object. 'It's white. It's—' He broke off and shrugged. 'Sophia, why do you keep pestering me like this?' he asked gently.

Kyle peered down at the old man. Mr Rostavitch was obviously a pretty smart old guy. Maybe he really was a retired professor or something. But why hadn't he just said that his wife was holding a coffee cup? Mr Rostavitch's response was definitely weird. But did it show that he had some kind of medical problem?

'It's like this with everything,' Mrs Rostavitch declared sadly. 'Ever since bedtime. I stayed up talking to him when I first noticed the problem, but I got so worried that I thought I should bring him in. It's terrible. He doesn't know what anything is anymore!'

Kyle looked at Mr Rostavitch. Then he glanced over at the empty couch across the room. 'Uh, sir, what's that over there?' he asked, pointing at the couch.

Mr Rostavitch squinted at it, then he smiled. 'It's very interesting!' he said. 'It's a brightly colored, large object. It has bulges all over it, funny-looking bulges, and I think it's made of something soft because—'

But Kyle had heard enough. Mrs Rostavitch was right. There was something very wrong here. 'I'll take you back to a cubicle right away,' Kyle said. 'And I'll see that our on-call physician has a look at you as soon as possible.'

'Thank you!' exclaimed Mrs Rostavitch, looking relieved.

But Mr Rostavitch tugged nervously at his beard. 'I don't want to go to a cubicle,' he protested. 'I don't want to see any doctors. I feel perfectly healthy.'

'You may feel perfectly healthy,' Kyle said soothingly, 'but it's a good idea to get checked out. Look at it this way, sir – at least it'll put your wife at ease.'

The old man's face softened. 'Oh, very well,' he said. 'Lead the way.'

Kyle noticed Mr Rostavitch had trouble finding his way to the cubicle. If his wife hadn't been there to guide him, he would have walked right into the walls! The old man definitely needed help.

Kyle grabbed his chart and went to find Dr Martinez. But Dr Martinez was busy with the man with angina, so Martha sent him over to the resident instead.

'There's a man who has something very strange wrong with him,' Kyle said. 'I think you should look at him.'

'What are his symptoms?'

Kyle hesitated. 'I don't know how to describe it,' he said, screwing up his eyes. 'He's – well, it's weird.

It's like he sees things, but he doesn't know what they are. He's sort of mixed up.'

'Is it some sort of psychiatric problem?'

'I don't think so,' Kyle replied.

'Why not?'

'He's not crazy, he just—' Kyle broke off, groping for words. Then he quickly told the resident about the coffee cup and the couch.

The resident's eyes widened. He whistled. 'Amazing. I've never seen a case like that. I've read about it, but I've never actually seen one before.'

'A case of what?' Kyle said.

'It's called *agnosia*,' the resident explained. 'At least, that's what it sounds like the patient has. A neurologist will have to be called in to make the final diagnosis, of course. But from what you've said, I'm pretty sure that has to be it.'

'But what *is* it?' Kyle burst out, feeling bad for Mr Rostavitch. He seemed like such a nice old man, and agnosia, whatever it was, sounded bad.

'It's a very rare side effect of a stroke,' the resident explained soberly. 'What happens is that the stroke damages the brain in such a way that the patient can no longer recognize objects despite adequate sensory information reaching the brain.'

'I wish you'd say that again in plain English.'

The resident smiled slightly. 'I know it's pretty hard to understand, but it's exactly what you saw. The patient could see objects and describe them in detail, but he couldn't tell you what they were or what they were used for.'

'That sounds like what's wrong with Mr Rostavitch,' Kyle admitted. 'But how can a person describe something so well and not be able to just say what it is?'

'You got me,' the resident admitted. 'But the human brain is a remarkable organ. Now you better show me to the patient.'

'Sure, right this way.' Kyle led the resident down the hall. As they walked, Kyle thought about how anxious Mrs Rostavitch had seemed. Now he understood why. Something very serious was wrong with her husband. Kyle couldn't imagine going through life not being able to identify even the simplest objects!

He glanced up at the resident. 'I was just wondering,' he said instantly, 'can you do anything to help him?'

'You mean to cure agnosia?' the resident asked. He shook his head. 'No, I'm afraid there's not much we can do except help the patient cope better with the problem. However,' he added as he stepped toward the cubicle, 'often with stroke victims, the damage repairs itself somewhat with time.'

Kyle nodded. He watched as the resident vanished

behind the curtain. Then he yawned. It must be almost four o'clock in the morning. Kyle couldn't remember ever feeling so wired and so exhausted at the same time.

'Just deal, bro,' he muttered, repeating Alec's old line out loud to himself. Then he shuffled back to the admitting desk, where Martha was waiting. Kyle noticed a brown paper bag was set on the side of the desk. A woman's handbag was laid neatly on top.

Regina's stuff, Kyle guessed, and then he winced. 'What do you need me to do now?' he said aloud.

'Go sit with the amnesia victim that was brought in earlier,' Martha replied, flipping through a stack of charts. 'They just brought her back from her CAT scan, and she's pretty agitated. You won't have to be with her for long,' the nurse added reassuringly. 'Dr Martinez just went upstairs to fetch the on-call neurologist to look her over. He should be back down here in five minutes, max.'

'No problem,' Kyle said.

The girl with amnesia was in the last cubicle on the right. Martha wasn't kidding that she was agitated. When Kyle stepped into the cubicle, the girl was sitting on the edge of the examining table, rocking herself back and forth. Tears spilled down her cheeks.

'Come on. Take it easy,' Kyle said. He'd never seen anyone look so totally heartbroken before. He sat down beside her.

'My head hurts,' the girl sobbed.

'It'll stop hurting soon,' Kyle assured her. 'The doctors will take care of it. You'll see.'

The girl looked up at him. 'But I don't belong!' she declared in a hopeless whisper.

A shiver went up Kyle's spine. 'What do you mean, you don't belong?'

'I don't belong! I don't belong anywhere!'

'You must belong somewhere.'

'I can't remember.' The girl hugged herself tighter. 'I keep trying. But no matter how hard I try to remember, there's no one. There's nothing!' Tears streamed down her face faster.

'Come on. Calm down. It's going to be okay.'

The girl just held her head and moaned. Kyle struggled not to yawn. He knew it would be horrible to yawn at a time like this, but he was so tired. 'I know you belong somewhere,' he said warmly.

The girl didn't move, but she stopped rocking herself to and fro. Her sobs got quieter. Kyle just sat there beside her. He didn't know what else to do. There wasn't anything else he *could* do until Dr Martinez came back with the neurologist.

The girl lifted her head. 'Where's my purse?' she suddenly asked in a different tone of voice.

'Your purse?' Kyle looked around. 'You didn't come in here with a purse,' he said, bewildered. 'You didn't come in here with anything.'

The girl blinked. 'But I want my purse.'

'What does it look like?'

The girl's eyes became more focused. 'It's brown leather,' she said slowly. 'It's a brown leather backpack with my monogram on it. J.J.'

'J.J.?' Kyle barely dared to breathe. 'What does J.J. stand for?' he asked, forcing himself to keep his voice even.

The girl began to sob again. 'Julia Johnson,' she wept. 'That's my name. Julia Johnson!'

Kyle knew he should probably ask for her address, keep her talking, but he was too overwhelmed. 'Wait right here,' he said breathlessly. 'I'm going to get the nurse.'

He dashed out to the waiting room, where Martha was showing a young man on crutches to a cubicle. 'Martha, the amnesia victim – she just remembered her name!' Kyle blurted. 'It's Julia Johnson!'

Only after the words were out of his mouth did Kyle realize how unprofessional he was being, rushing up and interrupting Martha like that. Surprisingly the nurse didn't scold him. She only said, 'Good work, Kyle. I'll be right there!'

Moments later, Martha, Dr Martinez, and the on-call neurologist were all gathered in Julia Johnson's cubicle. Kyle wished he was with them. He wondered if Julia could remember everything now that she had remembered her name. He knew it was none of his business – not really – but he couldn't help feeling strangely exhilarated.

He didn't think he'd ever forget the way the girl's eyes had suddenly focused, how she had suddenly come out with her name. He also would never forget how despairing she had sounded when he first went in to sit with her. *I don't belong. I don't belong anywhere.* That had to be about the saddest thing he had ever heard anyone say.

Carefully, Kyle finished stocking the last few supply cabinets in the ER. Things were pretty slow right then, but Kyle was determined not to slack off. Ms Dominguez had made it clear that this extra shift was a test for him, Kyle Cullen. And if he failed it, he was in big trouble. If Ms Dominguez didn't agree to write him a college recommendation, it might mess up his whole future. Tonight was a very big deal, in more ways than one. At the same time, Kyle thought wearily, what Ms Dominguez decided about him almost didn't seem to matter anymore. This shift was like nothing Kyle had ever been through. He didn't think he'd ever be the same.

'Just deal, bro,' he reminded himself.

He glanced over at the brown bag at the edge of the admitting desk. Regina's things. Regina who had been there one minute, and gone the next. No one had come to pick up the bag yet. Kyle blinked.

'Hey, don't pass out on us,' Martha said behind him.

Kyle turned around. 'What? I'm fine!'

'I know you're fine,' Martha said. 'You just look pretty wiped out, that's all.'

'I am, I guess,' Kyle admitted. 'This is the first time I've ever pulled a double shift.'

'Well, if you're as serious about medicine as you seem to be, it won't be the last,' Martha said. 'But I know how you feel. It's been a hard shift.'

'Well, at least only a few ambulances came in,' Kyle said.

'That's true.' Martha sighed. 'But it's been hard anyway.'

Kyle knew she meant Regina, and he nodded slowly. 'What happened with that girl – Julia Johnson?' he asked after a moment.

Martha smiled. 'We called her parents. They're on

their way over. Apparently, she's been missing for two days and they've been frantic. They sounded ecstatic when Dr Martinez called.'

'That's good.' Kyle rolled the supply cart into the corner. 'But what happened to her? I mean, why did she get amnesia?'

Martha's face darkened. 'It looks like it might have been a mugging,' she said, 'but I don't expect we'll ever know for sure. She has a severe concussion. The neurologist thinks it was caused by a blow to the head. Her purse is missing. The jewelry her parents say she was wearing is also gone – a couple of gold rings and a gold chain with a diamond pendant.'

'You're kidding!'

'No. The police are talking to her now, but she doesn't remember anything except being at school that afternoon, as usual. She goes to the French school downtown. I guess her parents are pretty wealthy. Anyway, she remembers the final school bell ringing, and after that, nothing.'

'Won't she remember sooner or later?'

'With injuries like that, the gap in memory is usually permanent,' Martha said. 'At least she remembers who she is now and where she's from. That means she's making a pretty fast recovery.'

'That's good,' Kyle said. He looked up at Martha.

'It was awful when I first went in to sit with her,' he said passionately. 'She was just crying and crying and saying how she didn't belong anywhere, she didn't have anyone.'

'Well, she does,' Martha said. 'She's lucky.'

'Yeah.' Kyle shook himself. 'So what do you want me to do now?' he asked. He was trying to keep his professional tone, but it was getting harder by the minute. His legs and arms ached, and his eyelids felt as heavy as bricks.

Martha shrugged. 'I don't know. You only have fifteen minutes left here, and it's pretty slow right now. Why don't you go get yourself a cup of coffee?'

'Are you sure there's not more restocking you want me to do first?'

Martha shook her head. 'No,' she said good-naturedly. 'You've done enough for one night. And don't worry,' she added, raising one eyebrow. 'I'll make sure to tell Ms Dominguez you did a good job here.'

'Thanks!' Kyle set off toward the coffee machine.

It felt odd not to have to do anything else. He'd been forcing himself to work so long that it didn't feel right not working. Plus not working just gave him more time to think about what a long night it had been – about Mr Rostavitch and Julia Johnson, and most of all about Regina. Kyle shuddered. Then he reached into his back pocket and pulled a slip of paper out of his wallet. On it was Alec's number at the hospital where he was staying. Kyle's mom had given it to him Friday morning and told him to call. But he hadn't. He'd felt too weird. Besides, lately Alec hadn't seemed like he wanted to talk to anyone – especially Kyle.

Kyle was about to put the number back in his pocket when he thought again of how nice Regina had been. Then he thought of the despair in Julia Johnson's voice when she said she didn't belong, when she said no matter how hard she tried she couldn't remember anything or anyone.

How would that feel? Kyle wondered. *How would it feel to think you were completely alone in the world?*

He pulled a quarter out of his pocket, went over, and fed it into the pay phone. He dialed Alec's number. 'Please deposit fifty more cents,' said the recorded voice of the operator. Kyle deposited two more quarters. Then another voice came on the line: 'Sunnyvale Clinic!'

'May I speak to Alec Cullen, please?'

'Who's calling?'

'It's his brother, Kyle.'

'Just a minute.'

It was only then that Kyle realized that it was 5:50 in the morning. *They must think I'm nuts calling so early,* he thought. *Alec probably isn't even awake!*

But then Alec's voice came on the line. 'Kyle, what are you doing up?'

Kyle stood up straighter. Alec sounded really glad to hear from him. 'I can't believe *you're* up,' he retorted.

Alec laughed. 'They make us get up early here. Very early. What's your excuse?'

'I worked a double shift at the hospital.'

'You like it that much?' Alec sounded a little jealous.

'Well, I got in trouble with the woman in charge.' Kyle told Alec the whole story. He could tell Alec was glad he was confiding in him, so he told him about the rest of the night – especially about Regina. 'I almost lost it,' he finished, 'but then I remembered what you always used to say: "Just deal, bro." '

Alec was silent a moment. 'I didn't know what I was talking about when I used to say that,' he said finally.

'It helped me.'

'Well, I'm glad it helped you. But I think I've learned that it isn't always that easy to "just deal." It can be pretty hard.'

'Yeah,' Kyle agreed. 'I never knew how hard.' He took a breath. 'So how are you doing there?'

'Better,' Alec replied quietly. 'A lot better. I still have a lot to work through, but I'm getting there. You know, sometimes admitting you really have a problem is the most important step to getting through it.'

'I can sure understand that.'

'So when am I going to see you, bro?'

'Soon,' Kyle promised. 'Next weekend, maybe.'

'That would be awesome,' Alec said.

'It sure would,' Kyle said, and he realized he meant it.

17

Max had spent the entire afternoon after school trying to get through to the testing service on the phone. She had kept hitting redial until she thought she'd go nuts. How could an 800 number be busy? She had finally gotten through, only to hear a recording that informed her that the current waiting time was fifteen minutes.

Max cradled the phone between her neck and shoulder and checked the clock. She had half an hour before she was due to leave for the hospital. What if the testing service closed and there was no one there to talk to? She anxiously checked over her calculus homework for the seventh time that afternoon. Finally, a voice answered the line.

'May I help you?'

'Yes, please. My name is Max Camacho,' she began. 'I took the SAT two weeks ago and something happened so that I couldn't finish the test. I was wondering if you could help me?'

'I can try. Social security number, please?'

Max gave her the number and waited. And waited.

'I'm just pulling up your file on our computer, but there's a note here,' the woman said. 'I'm going to have to go check your actual file. You can wait on the phone or we can get back to you.'

'I'll wait,' Max answered anxiously.

'It might be a few minutes.'

'No problem. This is really important to me.'

'I can hear that, Ms Camacho. Please hold.'

The minutes ticked by. Max gnawed on a hangnail and wished she had some food to munch on. She was anxiously hungry. This was the pits! Her guidance counselor had called the colleges she'd applied to, making sure they put a note in her files that her test scores might be arriving late. The admissions secretaries at both of her top choices told the counselor that Max would probably miss the last deadline, and that she should try to put a rush on the scores or she would have to wait until the following year to get admitted. The counselor hadn't had the heart to tell her that her test was probably untraceable since she had never even handed it in. What if the proctors had thrown it away last week? By the time she and Sara had gone back into the testing room, after the ambulances had left, everyone had been gone. Now her entire future was hanging on the line. At least they had her name in the computer.

'Ms Camacho?'

'Yes?' Max's heart was pounding.

'It says here that you never completed the test, is that correct?'

'Yes. But I have an explanation. I—'

'It's actually all here.'

'What?'

'There's a letter on file here.'

'There is?' Max asked. But how could that be? Her guidance counselor had not yet sent out her letter. 'Are you sure?'

'Yes, Ms Camacho. Someone mailed in the newspaper articles to us last week, explaining what had happened and making a request for special circumstances consideration on your behalf. The testing commission has decided to give you the benefit of the doubt, average out your scores on the other sections, and give you that average score for the section you failed to complete.'

'Really? Really?' Max was so excited she couldn't believe what she was hearing. Who could have sent in the articles? And who wrote the letter?

The lady continued. 'Yes, really. Do you have a list of the colleges you would like us to send your scores to?'

'I – yes! Hang on a minute, please!' Max cried. She dumped the phone on her bed and rummaged through the box with all her college information in it. 'Here.' She gave the woman the four-digit codes for the colleges she was applying to. 'And can I ask just one small favor? I know that you've already been great to me, but is there any way that these could be rushed?'

'It's ten dollars a school.'

'Oh.' Max did a quick calculation. 'Yikes.' Well, she'd just have to find the money somewhere.

'But in light of the extraordinary situation, I think I can manage to slip it through,' the woman confided.

Max could practically hear her smile through the phone. 'Thank you so much!' she said. 'I really appreciate it!'

'No problem. Your confirmation number is GMK–4408. Have a nice day.'

'You too!' Max hung up the phone. She had forgotten to ask who had sent in the articles. She must have a guardian angel somewhere. 'Yes! Yes! Yes!' she cried.

Her mother came rushing into her room. '*Qué pasó?* What happened?' she asked, her voice full of alarm.

Max grabbed her mother's arms and danced with her around the room. 'This is the best Christmas present ever! I think I just might make it to college after all!' she cried. Then she plopped down on her bed. 'Now all I have to do is hope my score averages out okay, get accepted, find scholarship money, finish my hundred hours of volunteering, and graduate with honors! Piece of cake,' she mumbled, realizing that the battle was not even a fifth over. 'Piece of cake.'

'Speaking of which,' her mother said in Spanish, 'are you hungry?'

'Am I ever!' Max bounded out of the room and followed her mother into the kitchen where she scarfed down two pieces of pound cake and a glass of milk while she told her mother what had happened. 'Someone sent them in on my behalf. I would never have thought of trying to do that. I wonder who it was!'

'The world works in mysterious ways,' her mother said wisely, nodding and crossing herself.

'Right, Mama.' Max brought her plate to the sink and grabbed her backpack. 'Got to run.'

'Don't you walk tonight, *mija*,' her mother warned. 'I want you to take the bus both ways.'

'But Mama, it's only ten blocks!'

'No buts!'

Max groaned and checked her watch. That gave her six minutes to make it to the bus stop. She ran out of the house and all the way to the bus stop, which was a block out of her way. It was so much easier to go straight to CMH on foot. But once it got dark, her mother was right. The neighborhood got kind of scary. There were lots of gangs and lots of people who just hung out on street corners looking to buy and sell drugs. Max had spent her whole life in this inner-city neighborhood, so she knew how to get around and how to avoid hassles, but being overly cautious never hurt. It just took time.

Max got on the bus and paid the driver. She was out of breath. The bus was nearly full of people returning home from work and kids coming home from school.

'Move to the back!' the bus driver ordered, pulling away sharply from the curb.

'I'm as far back as I can get,' Max mumbled, stumbling into a front seat as the bus careened into traffic. It was already dark outside and the traffic was filling the streets.

Max wondered what she was going to say to Dagger once she saw him. They had talked only once all week. She had spent most of her time thinking long and hard about what she should do. On one hand, Dagger's attention and dedication to his new job had shown a maturity and responsibility that she had never seen. While Gran Tootie recovered at home, Dagger was bringing in money so she wouldn't have to take on any work to support them. Mr Childs's tutoring was forcing him to study hard after long days at work and school. At Thanksgiving, he had even helped Reverend Bridges and his wife cook the turkey and all the fixings, and then helped them bring some to the hospital so that Gran Tootie still got to eat all her favorite holiday foods. He also took care of Gran Tootie in other ways, going so far as to wash and iron his own clothes for the first time in his life. He was being the man of the house. That was the good stuff. On the other hand, Max was pretty sure he was still dating that other girl.

The one thing Max didn't like thinking about was what Sara had suggested, which was that Max's jealousy might be blowing things out of proportion. Max herself couldn't understand why if she felt secure about so many other things, she could feel so insecure and jealous in a relationship with Dagger.

The driver slowly managed to advance a block and pulled over to the curb again to let passengers off. Max sighed. She could have been halfway to CMH already if she had just walked.

Staring out the window as the bus crept along in traffic, Max was grateful again for the testing service's generosity. She'd never heard of anything like that in her life, but then again, she hadn't ever been in the college-bound loop, so maybe kindness in academia was more common than she might expect.

Max thought about the fact that Sara was due to talk with her mom tonight. Totally strange not to have a mom around for years and then meet her when you were practically all grown-up. Max did not like Sara's mom for all the things she had done to Sara, but she was dying to hear how it would all come out.

A block from the hospital, the traffic seemed to open up. 'Finally!' Max grumbled, slipping on her volunteer shirt and clipping on her ID tag ahead of time. It was six o'clock and she was going be in trouble with Ms Dominguez for being late. She hated being late. Why did she have to listen to her mom about taking public transportation?

A hundred feet from the hospital and right in the middle of the lane, the driver slammed on the brakes, and Max suddenly lurched forward. She grabbed onto the seat in front of her and looked up. The driver was seated on the left side of the bus, three feet in front of her, craning forward. 'What the . . . ?' What was he looking at?

The bus driver turned off all the lights in the bus. The passengers went berserk.

'What's going on?'

'Hey! Let me out of here!'

'Turn on the lights, you freak!'

Max started to get up when she heard the driver

speaking urgently into his handheld radio. 'Marco! Marco! What's happening up there?'

Max craned her neck to see what the driver was looking at. In the bus ahead of them, there was something going on. Max tried to see.

'Marco! Answer me! Marco!' The driver sounded panicked.

Max could barely make it out in the dark. Inside the bus in front of them, two men were struggling. There was a flash. Max thought she heard the distant pop-pop of gunfire. So did other people on the bus.

'Let me out!'

'Hey! Open these damn doors!'

'*Abre la puerta!*'

'*Dios mio*,' swore the driver. He pulled the bus to the side of the street and addressed the passengers. 'Don't move! Everybody stay put! There's trouble up there.'

Crouched down, Max watched the other bus through the bar at the top of the seat. *Pop-pop-pop!* It was definitely gunfire. Max breathed deeply as she tried to make out what was going on. But she needn't have bothered.

The bus in front of them suddenly roared to life and sped forward. The whir of an approaching ambulance's siren was interrupted only by the ambulance's angry horn. Max watched in uncomprehending fascination as the speeding bus suddenly veered to the left. The screech of tires was almost as loud as the sound that followed of metal hitting pavement and sliding reluctantly across the street. Max was so horrified that she did not dare to blink or breathe. The sound of the ambulance siren was suddenly cut off. The bus, crunched on its side, had come to a halt. The street was completely quiet.

The silence did not last very long.

18

Dagger was actually right on time for once. He couldn't decide whether to hang out at the locker room and wait for Max or just see her up in the ER. He had spoken with her only once that week. She had told him she was still trying to 'sort things out,' whatever that meant. He had no idea what to expect from her tonight, but he was hoping that she was not going to tell him to take a hike forever. He had missed her more than he had expected to. He couldn't imagine the school Christmas break, only a week away, without at least some contact with Max.

He slipped on his shirt and clipped on his ID tag. He'd just go up to Ms Dominguez's office. He hopped up the stairs past a big, glittery poster announcing the staff Christmas party that night. He turned right, left, and there he was. Sara was already ahead of him and so was Kyle. Figured! Those two were always on time.

He greeted Ms Dominguez.

'Hello, Mr Fredericks.' It always blew his mind how formal Ms Dominguez was.

'Hey,' Dagger said, addressing both Kyle and Sara.

'You seen Max?' he and Sara both said to each other at the same time. They laughed.

'No,' Sara said. 'Have you, Ms Dominguez?'

Ms Dominguez shook her head. 'Not yet, I'm afraid.'

Dagger shrugged. 'She'll be here. She's no flake.'

Just then the phone rang. Ms Dominguez picked it up. 'Right away!' She hung up and turned to the volunteers. 'I don't know what's going on. That was Nancy. She asked me to come down in a hurry.'

The volunteers jumped to their feet and raced over to the ER, Ms Dominguez close behind. Nancy was leaning over the EMS computer, trying to make out the words through the static.

'Hello? Is this the county hospital? Is anyone there?'

'This is CMH. We read,' Nancy said. The volunteers stared at the screen. This was not normal ambulance talk.

'I need help. I'm inside—'

'Hey!' a man screamed across the ER. 'Quick! There's a huge accident down there right in front of the hospital. You have to come quick! And bring a lot of doctors! It's a rush hour bus filled with people and an ambulance – it's a mess! Quickly!' He ran out the doors through the ambulance bay.

Nancy turned back to the EMS computer. 'I'm sorry, I didn't catch that. Where are you?'

'I'm inside an ambulance. I broke my leg and they were taking me to the hospital. We got into an accident. I can't wake up the drivers! Hello! Are you there? Can you help me? My leg! My leg!'

'Don't panic,' Nancy said. 'We'll be right there to help you!' Nancy got onto the loudspeaker. 'All ER personnel to the admitting desk. All ER personnel to the admitting desk. All ER personnel to the admitting desk.'

A bunch of residents and a few interns rushed over. 'Outside!' she yelled. 'Right outside! There!' she repeated to their uncomprehending faces, pointing to the ambulance bay doors. They rushed out. More doctors and nurses came pouring into the ER. Dagger had never seen so many of them at once in one place.

Nancy handed the headset to another nurse. 'Take this! It's a patient in an ambulance that went down. See if you can keep him calm and find out where he is. You, Kyle! Get all nonurgent patients out of the interior waiting room and into the exterior, now! Sara, help him! Dagger, come with me!'

She dumped a pile of blankets into his arms and rolled out a crash cart stacked with first-aid supplies.

Dagger plopped the blankets atop another crash cart and followed Nancy out the doors of the ambulance bay. She was practically running. The carts clattering precariously, they ran into the bay and down the ramp toward the front of the hospital. At street level and on the front lawn of the hospital, Dagger could not believe what he saw.

'Mercy!' Nancy cried.

A huge city bus lay smashed on its side, the front end of an ambulance crushed into its undercarriage. A fire engine had just pulled up and firefighters were swarming the accident. Three police cars screeched to a halt, one after another. The officers swarmed out of their cars and tried to keep away the onlookers who were not hospital staff. The fire department was trying desperately to cut open the side of the bus near the windows now facing toward the sky. Dagger wondered if anyone was still alive. Then he heard the cries of people trapped inside the bus.

'What do we do?' he asked Nancy.

'Follow me with those blankets and that cart. No, better yet, go back and get some gurneys. Get the techs to help you. We're going to need plenty!'

Dagger glanced back at the smoking wreck and the area lit up by the circulating red lights of the emergency personnel, then took off. He ran up the ramp, passing several doctors and nurses rushing down to the site of the accident. Breathless, he pounded through the ambulance bay doors. On second thought, he pressed the lock that kept the doors open.

Sam spied him. 'What's going on out there, son?'

'It's a bus! And an ambulance. Right out front. I need gurneys. Can you get me some help?' Dagger managed to say.

'Right on it!' Sam said. He got on the loudspeaker. 'All orderlies to the ER. All orderlies to the ER.'

Dagger went over to the nurse on the EMS computer. He whispered to her, 'It's got to be the ambulance right out there. Tell the guy the paramedics are going to get him out of there any minute!'

She nodded and went back to the headset to relay the message to the person trapped inside the ambulance.

Four orderlies appeared. 'Out front!' Dagger pointed.

'Okay, let's line 'em up!' Each orderly went into a cubicle and pulled out a gurney. Dagger lined up the ones in the waiting area. They pulled two empty ones away from the walls. 'Get in the middle, like this!' one orderly said to Dagger. 'Hold on to each with one hand and that way you can pull two. Let's get a move on!'

They tugged the ten gurneys out the door just as Sam was directing more orderlies into the cubicles.

Dagger pushed and pulled, the metal bars hitting his legs painfully as they moved down the ramp toward the accident site. A doctor and a nurse ran past them with a kid in their arms. Another nurse helped a man walk unsteadily up the ramp. They must have gotten into the bus to rescue the passengers, Dagger realized. Good.

Down on the street there were bodies lying everywhere. One of the orderlies had thought to pile up more blankets onto the gurneys. Doctors grabbed at whatever supplies they could get their hands on. Interns and residents were on their hands and knees tending to patients sprawled out on the grass. There was no longer protocol or hierarchy, only the urgency of saving lives. If someone needed help, they received it, no matter the task.

'I need oxygen over here!' yelled a doctor who was kneeling over a man laid out on the pavement.

'Coming right up!' Dagger yelled. 'I'll be right back!' He inched himself out of the tangle of gurneys and sprinted back up the ramp. In the first Trauma Room he found two portable oxygen machines. He tried to pull out both but they were too heavy and unwieldy. 'Sam!' he called.

'I'll help you with that,' said a tech. 'Let's go!'

Both Dagger and the tech pushed the heavy

machinery out into the bay and rapidly down the ramp. Dagger was glad he had sneakers on because the weight of the machine was pulling him down the incline. The doctor already had the patient up on a gurney and he was doing CPR. 'I got a pulse! Get that oxygen on him and let's get him up to trauma. He's got a head wound. Looks like a bullet but I can't be sure!' An orderly and a resident pushed the gurney up toward the hospital.

Dagger's head was spinning as he tried to figure out what to do. Ellen O'Hara and another triage nurse were assessing the urgency of the injuries of the various passengers from the bus. They had neon reflective stickers that they stuck on visible parts of each patient.

'One of us has to go into the ER to keep it from getting crazy!' Dagger heard.

'I'll go up when we're done!' came Ellen's reply.

'Dagger! Over here!' It was Nancy. 'Go up to the supply closet and bring down as many towels and blankets as you can. There's no way we're going to get all these people up there right now. Only the immediates are being taken up right now! There aren't enough gurneys. You got that?'

She didn't wait for his reply. Dagger ran up the ramp again and into the ER. Slipping past the admitting desk, he slid into the supply closet. Kyle was on his heels. 'You need help?'

'Grab blankets and towels! Lots!'

Kyle and Dagger piled the supplies into their arms and Dagger ran out with Kyle right behind him. Dagger heard Kyle's intake of breath as they approached the wreckage on the street. 'No way!'

'Yes way! This way!' Dagger yelled. They threaded their way through the barrage of emergency personnel over to where Nancy was.

'Take one to each patient. I think they got them all out of the bus already. There should be at least one doctor or nurse to a patient. Start with the red stickers and then go to the blues. They'll tell you what to do.'

Kyle and Dagger split up. Dagger went to the first patient with a red sticker that he saw. It was a man who appeared unconscious. 'Blanket?'

The nurse grabbed it and continued to take his pulse. 'Damn!' he heard her curse. 'I've got no pulse here! Will someone please bring me the oxygen?' Dagger dropped the blankets where he stood and went to fetch the machine at the perimeter of the crowd. He raced back with it as the nurse and a resident lifted the man onto a gurney. 'Airway clear. No pulse. Not breathing,' he heard her say as they raced past him. 'Well get it up there!' she yelled at Dagger.

A doctor rushed up to him. 'You need this, son?'

Dagger shook his head.

'Good.' The doctor whisked the oxygen machine away.

Dagger found the pile of abandoned blankets and handed them out. *There must be fifty people on the ground,* he thought. Kids, grown-ups – it was the biggest pile of misery he had ever seen. People were wailing and calling out to family members. The scene was crowded with medical personnel. The grass was lit up with street lights and police lights, casting eerie shadows on the nighttime scene.

As he passed the back of the ambulance, the firefighters were pulling a man out of it. They had managed to slip a backboard under him and a cervical collar circled his neck. 'My leg!' he yelled.

'You're going to be all right,' said a fire department paramedic.

'What about the drivers?' the man cried. Dagger recognized his voice from the EMS call.

Dagger saw the paramedic and the firefighter exchange glances. 'Don't worry about them. We've got to get you into the ER right now. Hang on there.'

Dagger couldn't help but look at the front of the ambulance. There were two bodies laid out, both covered with hospital sheets. They were dead. Dagger could see from the bottoms of the sheets that they were wearing the regulation black-soled shoes of most EMS personnel.

'Those are the ambulance drivers,' Kyle said.

'Are you sure?'

'Yeah, I heard one of the firefighters. I have to run back.' Kyle took off toward the ER. *Probably to get more supplies,* Dagger thought. He headed over to a doctor doing CPR on a woman. A portable monitor was hooked up to her already. Its red light glowed eerily in the darkness intermittently punctuated by the whirling lights of the cop cars.

'I show a V-fib!' the doctor said, pressing down on the woman's chest again and again.

'Okay, Dan, clear out!' said another doctor, picking up the paddles of a portable defibrillator. He pressed the paddles against her chest. 'Clear?'

'Clear!' The body jerked.

'Anything?'

'No!'

'Do it again. Up it fifty joules!'

'Clear?'

'All clear!' The woman's body jerked again.

'Come on, sweetheart!' the doctor yelled. 'Come on!'

'Start the IV!'

'Epi-bolus!'

'Nothing!'

'Lidocaine!'

'Damn! I lost all rhythm on the monitor!'

'Clear?'

'All clear!' The body jerked again.

'How high are you?'

'Three-sixty!'

'Try four hundred!'

'Clear?'

'Clear!' The body jerked again.

'Any rhythms?'

'Nothing! Damn!'

Dagger walked away. He couldn't help and he couldn't bear to watch. It was awful. There were people screaming and yelling everywhere. He caught sight of a news camera shooting the scene. Until that moment he thought it was cool to be on the news. Now he thought those camera guys were just scum. How could they show real stuff like this to people on the news? It was terrible.

Dagger heard someone call for a volunteer. He looked around. Where was it coming from? He heard it again and looked to his left. A patient was calling out for a volunteer! He rushed over in the direction of the voice. How did they know... ?' Then he got confused, the lights in his face disorienting him.

'Over here! Dagger!' came the voice.

That's when he saw her. 'Max!' She was leaning over someone. 'You okay? You were late. I was getting worried—'

'I know, Dag. I saw the accident happen. I never checked in. Listen, I know this girl. She's pregnant. We have to get her a doctor!'

Dagger looked down. A young woman who looked their age was on her side, clutching her belly. She looked pretty pregnant to Dagger, though he had no idea how far along she was. 'Don't move!' Dagger ordered. He ran over to an empty gurney and snatched a blanket off.

'Hey!' yelled a nurse. 'I need that!'

'So do I,' Dagger yelled.

'Is your patient going in?'

'Not yet, I – I don't think!' he stuttered.

'Okay. Take it!' She looked grim as a woman was lifted onto her gurney and she and a resident pushed her toward the ER.

'Thanks!' Dagger yelled and ran off. He ran to where Max was, but she was gone. Where was she? His head was whirling.

'Dagger!' A resident and a tech had lifted the pregnant girl onto a gurney.

Dagger ran over to Max, his heart pounding. 'Here's your blanket.'

Max leaned over the gurney, speaking in Spanish. '*Estamos aqui. No te preocupes. El médico te va cuidar.*'

The girl nodded, then groaned and clutched her belly.

'She's going to be all right, miss,' the tech said. 'But we have to get her inside.'

Max moved back and watched as the girl was secured to the gurney. Suddenly Dagger wanted to hug Max – he was so glad to see her unhurt amidst all the wreckage.

'Can I go with her?' Max asked.

'Yes. In fact, you want to push her in? We have more urgent work to do over here.'

Max nodded and took the gurney. Dagger took the other end. Without saying a word, the two of them raced toward the ramp leading up to the ER, careful not to run over any lingering bodies on the ground, alive or dead.

Inside the ER, there were wall-to-wall people. Max stayed with the gurney as Dagger made his way through the throng to Nancy. 'Got a pregnant woman. She's—'

'Is she bleeding?' Nancy interrupted.

'I don't know.'

'See Ellen. She'll assign priority!' Nancy said and turned away.

Dagger looked around. Where in the heck was Ellen O'Hara? There were people groaning and doctors yelling. Someone near the ambulance bay doors was trying to usher people to the right and the left, into cubicles and rooms with a bullhorn. It was the other triage nurse he had seen earlier.

'Wait here!' he yelled to Max, who just nodded. She was holding the girl's hand, trying to comfort her.

Dagger wended his way through the crowd and over to the woman. She was about to shush him until she saw his shirt. 'What do you have?'

'You triage?'

She nodded.

'A pregnant woman.'

'She bleeding?'

'How am I supposed to know?'

'She in delivery?'

Dagger stared at her helplessly. Was this woman psycho or what? He wasn't a doctor. He shook his head. 'I really don't—'

'Where is she?' The nurse was obviously going to have to see for herself.

Dagger led her to the gurney. He and Max watched

as the nurse lifted up the blanket, gave the girl a quick check, and tagged her gurney with an immediate sticker.

'Take her over there. Chuck'll take her up to the third floor. She's not delivering right this second. They can take care of her up in the maternity ward.' Dagger followed Max.

The two of them waited until the girl was picked up. Sara came running over from the patient waiting area.

'Max! Did you really see what happened?'

'Man, it happened so fast I'm not even sure!' Max said. 'All I know is that I saw two guys wrestling in the bus ahead of us. Then there was gunfire, the bus accelerated, and crashed into the ambulance! I just jumped off my bus and ran to help.'

'Did you get a good look at anybody on the bus?' asked a voice behind them.

Dagger turned to face two police officers. Sara stepped back.

'No. Sorry. But if I think of anything, I'll let you know.'

The officers took down Max's name and left.

Dagger split up from the girls and went outside again. He spent the next while helping rush the last of the gurneys into the ER. Once the triage nurse assigned the urgents to various rooms of the hospital or ER, he helped the techs transfer each one to a hospital bed and then ran out again with the gurney. He did this until all the urgents were taken inside.

Half an hour later Dagger was returning from the blood lab with a heavy cart full of blood products. He delivered them to the various cubicles and rooms Nancy indicated. There was a hurried order to the chaos around him. He didn't understand how the ER managed to do it.

'Hey, how come the computer's quiet?' he asked Nancy, who, as usual, was barely sweating. The EMS computer was totally silent.

'They're rerouting all the emergencies to smaller hospitals in the area. We're simply too overloaded,' Nancy explained. She picked up the ringing phone. 'County ER. Yes, ma'am. I'll connect you.' She pressed the hold button. 'Dagger, see if you can get Max to go over to the Patient Relations office. They need a volunteer in there for fifteen minutes while Sandra takes a bathroom break! The phones are ringing off the hook with people calling about the accident. Then if you see Kyle, tell him to work on supplies. Oh! But first have Max go with you to get some supplies from the basement. We're low on towels. Have Kyle see Connie for the rest of the urgent supplies. 'Then Max can go up to Patient Relations.'

Dagger didn't stop to wonder how he had become head volunteer seeker-and-finder, but he raced off to locate Kyle and Max. Kyle he sent over to Connie's desk.

Max rounded the corner holding a stack full of towels. 'How did you know, you angel?' he said with a grin.

Max chuckled. 'ESP. Now help me put these on that cart – whoa!'

Dagger grabbed the top of the stack as it was about to topple to the ground. Max and he both had their arms around the towels when Dagger heard his name being called.

'Dagger!' a voice called out. 'Dagger! Is that you?'

Dagger turned and gulped. There was Kyra, and she was coming toward him with a worried look on her face.

'How did you get in here? What are you doing here?' he demanded. Why did this chick have just about the worst timing in the universe? Why? And why was she so damn beautiful?

'I just told them my father was a patient and they let me in! Man, it's a mess out there! Did you see that accident? I can't believe – oh!' She stopped herself, looking at Dagger. He realized that his hand was resting possessively on Max's arm.

'Are you busy or something?' Kyra asked testily.

'Kyra, I can't talk to you right now,' Dagger said. He could feel Max's eyes burning on him. He looked down at Max's face. She was expressionless. Like a rock. She turned her face away from them both. Something caught in Dagger's throat. It was painful, like a throb and a stab all at once. He inhaled and spoke again. 'As a matter of fact, this is my girlfriend.'

Kyra looked at Max. 'Your *what*?'

Max must have caught sight of Sara because Dagger saw her motion her over. 'Would you please take these towels over to the nurses' supply station by cubicle thirteen?' Sara nodded and pushed the cart away without even asking. That's when Dagger knew he was in for it. They were all ganging up on him.

'Excuse me?' Kyra said, flipping her long hair back. 'I thought you said you were single! Where did she come from? And *when*?'

Dagger looked at Kyra's angry face. Then he looked at Max; she didn't look all that thrilled, either. There were two angry women in front of him and both looked ready to kill him. What was he going to do?

'Is she like an ex or something?' Kyra demanded.

Dagger didn't know Kyra that well, but he had never seen this side of her. She was flaming mad. 'Well, it's actually more complicated, but . . .'

Max put her hands on her hips and looked up at Dagger. She raised her eyebrows infuriatingly. She was not about to jump in and help him, that much was clear.

'But what? Did you tell her about us?' Kyra shot back.

Sara came up behind Max, just as Dagger saw Max's eyes close. It was all over. He was going to lose her for good. His chest started to ache. 'What us? We went on one date—' he protested.

Kyra interrupted him. 'Is she your girlfriend or am I? That's the question I want answered. I don't have to put up with this. I could have a million guys.'

She was right, she could; Dagger knew that much from the first time he laid eyes on her. He looked at the two women in front of him and took a big breath. One of them he loved. The other he did not. Suddenly it was clear. 'Then maybe you ought to go be with one of them,' he said to Kyra in a low voice. 'I'm sorry.'

Kyra's face fell. 'Oh – I – uh – I—' she stuttered. 'Well, I guess you lose, loser.' She took one last look at Dagger, made a stony face at Max, and flounced out.

No one said anything for a cool minute. Dagger felt his body burst out into a belated sweat.

'Well,' Max said finally, 'she didn't put up much of a fight for you.'

Dagger saw Sara smirk and he winced. He looked at Max, fully expecting her to turn her back on him and walk away. But she didn't. She was just standing there, looking at him expectantly. 'What did you mean by "my girlfriend"?' she asked. Her voice was not challenging, but curiously tender.

'Don't you have some . . . supplies or something to go help with?' Dagger said to Sara.

'No, that's Kyle's specialty, as a matter of fact,' Sara deadpanned.

Max giggled. 'Go, girl!'

Sara paused. 'Okay, fine. But I'll be back. Will you be all right, Max?'

'Of course,' Max replied. 'So?' She was looking straight at him.

'Well, I still think of you as my girl, I guess,' he replied.

'Me and how many other girls?'

'That was nothing! I swear! She came in here chasing after me! I—' But Max's eyes were narrowed into little slits. She was clearly not buying it anymore. He sighed and began again. 'That's over. You're the one I really care about, Max. Honest.' His heart was beating crazily. How was he going to get her to believe him?

She stared at him a few moments longer. 'Dagger, I've been thinking. Remember what you said to me about my accepting you the way you were and not judging you? When I admitted that I didn't even know what I wanted in the future?'

Dagger nodded.

'Well, I realized you were right. I don't necessarily know the right way for both of us. I can only make my own decisions. I also really do like the *person* you are. And I'm liking what you *do* as that person more and more these days . . .'

He stared at her while her words sunk slowly in.

'And I really miss you.'

Dagger closed his eyes and lowered his head to her ear. 'Max,' he whispered. 'I . . . I love you. Okay?' He stood up again and wished he could fall into a hole. He had never said that aloud to anyone. Not even Gran Tootie.

Max beamed. 'Just for that little courageous act, *maybe* I'll give you another chance. But you have to promise that you're not going to interfere with my studies or try to get me to flake on my soccer games in the spring.'

'Max, I doubt I'm going to even have the time to talk you out of anything!'

'Swear?'

'Swear!'

Max smiled triumphantly.

Dagger suddenly slapped his forehead. 'Oh, no! I forgot! You're due up at Patient Relations!'

Max grinned. 'Right. See you later.' She walked off without a backward glance.

Dagger smiled and sighed. Women. Why was it they always ended up with the upper hand? Even when they sounded like they were cutting you a fair deal, they were always holding back the joker. It was beyond him. But he didn't care this time. Max might be a little bossy, but she was worth it. For the first time in weeks, Dagger felt lucky.

And even if she never did figure out that it was he who had sent in those articles to the college testing board, he decided he was not going to tell her. It would be his little secret – his little good deed for the year.

19

Sara walked away from Dagger and Max wishing she were a fly on the wall. Those two were like a soap opera. She had just finished helping Kyle with the last of the urgent supply errands when she was seized with a feeling of utter panic. Her mother was coming tonight! She had been totally grateful for the crazed activity of the bus and ambulance accident on CMH's front lawn. If she had taken time to think about what was about to happen, she would surely faint. Of course, she could always bail out, send Max in to say that she had to leave suddenly. But no, Max was still in the other room with Dagger.

Sara walked back into the ER, checking her watch. Only a little while to go until she saw her; Sara wondered if her mother was already in the cafeteria waiting for her. The ER was packed with doctors and nurses and gurneys. Luckily, most of the gurneys were now empty or filled with nonurgents with less critical injuries. Nancy and Ellen were sending the patients off one by one with teams of doctors and residents on other floors in the hospital since the ER was still filled.

Sara approached Nancy. 'How can I help?' she said simply.

'I'd like you to go outside where Kyle is and see if you can help with the last of the stragglers out there. There's nothing urgent left, but I'm sure they could use help with' – she mouthed the last words – 'the bodies.'

Sara grimaced.

'Sorry, we need all the skilled help right here.'

Sara had no choice. She made her way down the ramp. The accident site was still teeming with activity, but the doctors and nurses were all inside. Detectives took statements from onlookers, and police officers pushed the crowds outside of the yellow police tape. A tow truck was pulling the ambulance back from the undercarriage of the bus and the separation of inter-twined metal screeched like tractor claws being scratched down a steel backboard.

'The firefighters were milling around, cleaning up the spilled oil and gathering up the equipment they had used to pry the live patient with the broken leg out of the back of the ambulance. As Nancy had warned, bodies covered in plastic lay lined up side by side. There were four of them. No telling how many inside the hospital were already on their way to the morgue.

Kyle was nowhere to be seen, but Sara caught sight of Ms Dominguez and walked slowly over to her, being careful not to trample on the scattered pieces of rubber and glass that littered the blocked-off street. 'Want to help me?'

Sara gulped.

'I didn't think so. Sorry, but—'

'No problem,' Sara replied, surprised at the note of apology in the usually stern volunteer coordinator's voice.

Ms Dominguez motioned to two orderlies standing nearby. 'There's one for each of us. You two guys load 'em and we can all take one down to the morgue.' Sara watched as the orderlies each grabbed an end of a body in a dark-colored bag and hefted it onto a gurney. They did this three more times, the bodies landing with dull thuds on the white sheets of the gurneys. Sara jumped a bit each time. She felt like she could feel them landing, feel the air pushing out of their lungs as if they had been hit in the back. But they were dead. They couldn't feel, she reminded herself.

Sometimes Sara wondered if being a doctor was

the right career for her. But then she thought of how much she loved helping people get well. The idea of working as a psychiatrist was sounding better all the time. Unlike other mental health personnel such as psychologists or social workers, psychiatrists went to medical school. Then they tried to use their scientific and medical training along with their psychology backgrounds to help patients with emotional problems. It seemed to Sara like a good approach – taking into consideration the body as well as the mind. They were so intertwined. A sick body could be helped by a healthy mind. And a troubled mind could make a person's body ill. The primary bonus to psychiatry was twofold: Sara would be able to make people better, and she wouldn't have to cut into their bodies.

'Let's go!' Ms Dominguez said, interrupting Sara's reverie. She had just signed some papers for the detectives, who were releasing the bodies.

All four of them pushed bodies up the ramp toward the ambulance bay. Sara wondered how they were going to maneuver around the crowded waiting area. Wouldn't all the patients see the covered bodies and know they were dead?

Ms Dominguez, in the lead, steered them toward a locked entrance. She turned a key in the hole and a freight elevator opened up. It was wide enough for all four of the gurneys. The doors closed behind them and with another turn of the key on the panel, the elevator descended a floor. The opposite doors opened to the basement floor and Sara followed them out. They rolled the gurneys down the hall to the steel doors of the morgue.

Ms Dominguez pressed a button and brought her mouth to the speaker. 'This is Chelly. We have four more.'

'Open sesame,' said a cheery voice. The steel doors made a sucking sound and parted from the middle, revealing the large room with metal drawers from floor to ceiling on two walls.

Ms Dominguez pushed in her gurney and the others followed.

'Hi, Chelly! How's it going?' said the woman dressed in a long, white lab coat.

'Hi, Selene,' Ms Dominguez replied.

'These from the accident in front?' Selene asked.

'Yes. Listen, Selene, everything okay here?' Ms Dominguez asked, handing her the paperwork for the four dead bodies.

'A-okay!' Selene said, scanning the paperwork. 'Can't wait to get at 'em!'

Ms Dominguez smiled and led Sara and the orderlies out.

'Ms Dominguez? Can I ask you a favor?' Sara asked.
'Hmmm?'

'I . . . uh, I asked someone to meet me here tonight for a few minutes in the cafeteria. Do you mind if I take a fast break now? I should only be about fifteen minutes or so.' Sara was fumbling with her words. She almost wished Ms Dominguez would deny her permission so she wouldn't have to go.

'You've done a fine job tonight, Ms Greenberg. And I know that none of you have had a break, so go ahead. You'll only have half an hour more anyway before you're due to call it quits.'

'I know, I just didn't want you to think I was slacking,' Sara said. 'I know how busy it's been . . .'

When she had phoned her mother last week, she had asked her to stop by the hospital and meet her at the cafeteria for her last break of the night. She had not wanted to commit more time than that. They had not talked about anything else.

So when Ms Dominguez walked away, Sara felt her heart begin to pound – hard. What would her mother look like after six years? What if she was lying in her letter? What if she was still a drunken witch?

Sara walked into the cafeteria. It was nearly deserted, but looked more cheerful than usual because of all the Christmas and Hanukkah decorations everywhere.

She hesitated in the doorway underneath yet another poster about the staff Christmas party that night. She halfway hoped her mother would not have waited. But there she was, in the corner, sipping a soda. She rose upon seeing Sara and smiled. 'Hi.'

Sara didn't reply. Her mother looked different. Her hair was cut short like a boy's and colored a reddish-brown instead of her usual black. It softened the high-cheekboned face, but could not erase the wrinkles that lined the eyes and the mouth. She was dressed in beige slacks and a cream-colored blouse. A camel hair coat rested on her shoulders. She appeared professional – different from how Sara remembered her. She also looked much older than she had six years ago. Or maybe Sara had just not noticed her age until this minute.

'I know, I look older, don't I? I'm not even forty yet, but I look my age. You, on the other hand, look just as lovely as I knew you would.'

Sara felt mildly annoyed. Her mother was acting too familiar with her. She was a stranger. Well, almost. 'I'll, uh, be right back,' Sara said, her words sounding mechanical and shaky. She went to get something to drink. On the way over to the machine and back, her mind was a whirl of anxiety. *Calm down*, she told herself. *She's not going to hurt you. Not anymore.*

'Sara,' her mother said upon her return, 'I know you're upset at me. And you have the right, absolu—'

'Oh, please!' Sara said angrily. 'You've had no part in my life for the last six years and now you think we're going to be friends all of a sudden? I don't think so.' She couldn't believe how mad she felt. Her whole body was trembling. She tried to sip her soda but she wasn't thirsty.

Her mother searched her face. She was quiet for a few moments.

'What?' Sara said. 'Why are you looking at me like that?'

'I'm just marveling at how grown-up you look. And I'm trying to think of what I can say to you to make you feel better. But I'm not sure where to start. I'm overwhelmed, too. I've thought about this so many times, and yet I seem to be drawing a blank. Can we start with the fact that I am so sorry? Can we start with my apology to you?'

Sara did not reply for a second. She felt her hands twitch and unwanted tears spring to her eyes. She didn't trust herself to reply. 'That would be a good start,' she said at last.

'I'm so sorry, Sara. I was a rotten mother and an even more rotten person. I was never really there for you and when I was, I was a miserable drunk. And then to top it all off, I left you all alone. I can't begin to apologize enough. I'll spend the rest of my life wishing I could do it all over again. I'm different now, but I can't change the past, and neither can you. I'm so sorry, Sara. Truly.'

Sara looked up at her mother through her own tears and saw that her mother was also crying. She looked suddenly more *human* to Sara than she ever had before. She wasn't this mysterious bad memory. She was human.

Her mother spoke again. 'But we might be able to start on the future, on today. If you want . . . ?' She reached out a hand.

Sara looked at the hand but did not touch it. 'I don't know,' she finally replied. 'I don't trust you. I don't even know if I believe you . . .' Sara paused, then added quietly, not looking at her mother, 'But I wish I could.' When she looked up she saw that her mother's face had brightened.

'I understand. That's a start, I know it is. Maybe we can just start right there. Just as long as you want to, that's all I need to know. I can sit here for as long as you want, whenever you want, and try to help you believe me.'

'What if I can't forgive you right away?' Sara said in a small voice. 'I feel like you totally betrayed me.'

'I did. Your feelings are valid,' her mother admitted, her face full of pain.

'Did you really stop drinking?' Sara felt the stir of hope in her chest.

'Yes,' her mother replied softly. 'I did. And I've been clean for two and a half years – the longest in my entire life, that I can remember.' Her mother sounded proud to her, and a little hopeful.

'What about smoking?'

'Smoking, too. And I have a job and live in this little pink house in Tucson. It looks like a birthday cake. I work at an accounting firm, and I'm studying to get my CPA's license. Aren't you going to college soon?'

'I hope so,' Sara replied evenly. 'I find out in a few months. I was trying to improve my scores on the SAT, but something happened and I didn't finish the test, so I've just decided to go with the score I've got and hope for the best. I really want to go to school out of state, but you know my – you know Dad. He's going to be hard to convince.'

'Yes, your father always did think you were the light of his life. No matter what I think of him, I am thankful that you had a least one sane parent who knew how to show you love in the way you needed.'

Sara was surprised at the fact that her mother was

245

being so straightforward. She never remembered her being that way before. Maybe she *had* changed. The old Rachel never said she was wrong. The old Rachel blamed others and avoided responsibility. It was Sara, the child, who had been the responsible one. Her entire life, she had felt like she had to take care of her mother. Now her mother was acting like a real grown-up. It was sort of nice for a change, she realized.

'So are you going back to Tucson?' Sara asked.

'Well, that's up to you,' her mother replied.

'What do you mean?'

'It really depends on you. I can stay for a few days' – she paused, picking up on Sara's panic – 'or I can come back for a weekend when you're ready to spend some more time.'

Sara was silent. This was all moving a bit fast for her. She had so much else going on in her life. How was she supposed to spend her weekends talking to her mother? She felt guilty for thinking only about herself, and she felt righteous for doing so, as well. Most of all, she felt overwhelmed.

'Listen, Sara, you're in charge here. You don't have to do anything you don't feel comfortable with. If you just want to meet here once in a while, I can do that. Short visits until you're ready for more – if you are. It's up to you. I'm grateful that you agreed to meet with me at all.'

Sara looked at her mother. Her face revealed a sincere openness Sara had never seen before. She realized that she really wanted to believe her. 'How about you call me Thursday nights and we can decide about meeting on the weekends for lunch or something casual? That way it's not like an obligation,' Sara admitted. 'Not that I don't want to, but I'd just feel better that way.'

Rachel smiled. 'No problem. Whatever you want. And if you're not home, I'll leave you a message on your machine and you can call me back collect. And . . . you're also going to have to talk to your father about this sometime.'

Sara blanched. 'What do you mean?'

'Well, you're living under his roof, in his house. I don't want you lying or getting in trouble because of me. If you want me to talk to him—'

'No! I'll do it when I'm ready,' Sara broke in. 'I'll tell him . . . when there's something to tell. Just let me handle it.'

'That's fine. However you want to deal with it is fine. You're right. You're a young woman now and I can accept your decisions. I'll be happy to meet you whenever you have a chance.'

Sara looked at her watch. It was a quarter to midnight. She was late getting back to the ER. 'Listen, I have to go. I'm late.' She didn't know what else to say. She stood up and her mother rose, as well.

'Thank you, Sara,' she said appreciatively. 'Thank you for your generous heart. I'll try not to let you down again. I promise.'

Sara nodded. 'Okay, well, then, I – um, I'll talk to you on Thursday,' she stuttered.

'Great. Take care, Sara,' her mother said.

'You too, M—' Sara mumbled. She realized that she was about to add *Mom*, but she ate the end of her sentence.

It didn't get past her mother who simply said again, 'Thank you, Sara.'

Sara tried a tentative smile and turned toward the door. It all felt so unreal. She felt woozy and faded. It was like a dream. This woman was like a dream, nothing like the mother she remembered. And that was a good thing. A very good thing.

Sara waited for the elevator to take her back to the ER. She remembered that Hanukkah was just a few days away. For the first time in six years, she wouldn't have to wonder where her mother was. She wouldn't be hoping against hope that one of the wrapped gifts or unopened cards would be from her missing mother.

Even though she had no idea what was going to happen with her mother, she felt like she had been given an early gift for the holidays. It made her feel more peaceful inside than she had felt in many years.

20

Kyle had finally left the scene of the accident in front of CMH. The bus had been lifted by cranes onto the back of a wide flatbed eighteen-wheeler and the towing company was still securing it. The crushed ambulance had been towed away moments before. The firefighters had left the scene. Only the detectives, a few straggling onlookers, and a me-too, last-minute television crew were still on the scene. They had tried to interview Kyle, but he had found himself shaking his head and telling them that he had no comment. He just hadn't felt right. All his life he had wanted to be interviewed on TV, but when the opportunity had arisen, he had backed down, surprising himself as well as his coworkers.

Kyle walked up the ramp pushing an unusually light crash cart that had been plundered of its contents. As soon as the streets were swept up, no one would be able to tell that people had died out there only hour before. Again he thought of how, in a split-second, someone's life could change – or end – without warning. This made him think of Alec again, staying at a mental institution so that he wouldn't hurt himself. It was horrible. But Kyle felt better about it since talking to Alec. Alec was starting to sound more like his old self again. Of course, he wouldn't be able to tell for sure until he saw Alec this weekend, but Kyle had a feeling Alec would make it through this. Like his parents, he was hoping that Alec would be home for Christmas in a week or so. It was the first Christmas in his life that Kyle had not wished for something material, something that could be bought. All he wanted was for Alec to come home, the sentencing to be over and finished, and for his family to get back to normal – even though normal was far from perfect, it was sure better than the way things had been in his house lately.

He wended his way though the ambulance bay and into the ER. The place was no longer a veritable madhouse. All the accident patients were being attended to – they had all filled in admitting forms and were on their way into cubicles or already there. Kyle glanced out over the now quiet waiting room. A forlorn Christmas tree sat crookedly in the corner, next to a poster advertising some Christmas party.

Kyle let out a breath. The family members of the bus accident victims were no longer lined up in the exterior waiting room, but had been attended to by the Patient Relations staff.

Kyle checked his watch and saw that it was nearly midnight. Saturday he would go see Alec. Then on Sunday, he had a seminar to attend at the hospital. When Ms Dominguez had assigned him a seminar to help him deal with his time management problem, he had no idea that she would be teaching it. He had learned that in addition to running the volunteer program, she also taught classes in CMH's nursing program. Between his extra hours in the ER last week and this seminar, he felt like he practically lived at the hospital. And surprisingly – or maybe not so surprisingly – he found that he rather enjoyed it.

Kyle pushed the empty crash cart into the supply closet near the ER's admitting desk. He would fill it up as his last duty for the evening. He ran into Max and Dagger coming out of the kitchen. Sara was just finishing up with a patient chart that she handed to Nancy.

'It's midnight. You guys leaving?' Kyle asked.

Max, Dagger, and Sara all looked at each other. 'Aren't you planning to come to the party?' Sara asked.

'What party?' Kyle replied, looking confused.

'The staff Christmas party, Kyle,' Nancy cut in. 'It's starting upstairs in the third-floor nurses' lounge.'

'You're kidding!' Kyle exclaimed. 'How come nobody told me about it?'

'No one told anyone about it,' Max answered. 'There are posters advertising it everywhere you look.'

'Oh.' Kyle remembered the poster he'd seen in the hallway. He'd been so busy that he'd never bothered to look at the time or the date. 'Isn't midnight kind of late for a staff party?' he asked weakly.

'Not for us night owls here at CMH,' Nancy retorted.

Sara smiled at him. 'So you coming?'

Kyle hesitated. 'Sure, I guess.' He wasn't expecting to go to a Christmas party right that moment. But now that he thought about it, going to a party sounded like a great idea. He was so wired from the shift that even if he went straight home to bed, he'd never be able to get to sleep. 'Let me just call my folks – you know, tell them I'll be home late.'

'All right.' Nancy nodded approvingly. 'Why don't you just meet us upstairs?'

'Great.' Kyle waved and headed over to the pay phones.

A few minutes later, he was walking into the third-floor nurses' lounge. He could see why the ER staff had decided to hold the party up there. This lounge was a lot bigger than the cramped ER nurses' lounge downstairs. It was also much nicer-looking. The furniture actually matched and the rugs weren't covered in coffee stains. And what made it look even more festive were all the holiday decorations hanging up everywhere – ropes of tinsel, and paper Santa Clauses and menorahs. In the corner was a long table piled with food and drink. Kyle's mouth dropped open. It was a fantastic spread – there were plates of cheese and meat, smoked salmon, all kinds of dips and vegetables, and at least a dozen different kinds of cookies and cakes.

'Pretty sweet, huh?' Max murmured happily beside him.

'Yeah,' said Kyle in amazement. 'I never would have thought the cafeteria staff could make food like this!'

'They didn't,' Connie said behind him. She wrinkled up her nose. 'I guess the doctors are as sick of cafeteria food as we are. They all chipped in and hired an outside caterer.'

'I knew this food couldn't have come out of the cafeteria kitchen!' Max declared, wolfing down some cheese and crackers. 'This stuff actually tastes good!'

'*Real* good!' said Dagger, who was standing next to her, one arm draped around her shoulders while the other took some dip with a carrot stick.

Max grinned up at him. The way she grinned, Kyle figured the two of them must have made up in a big way. He was glad. He really liked Max and Dagger. And despite their troubles, Kyle had a feeling the two of them were really good for each other.

Kyle picked up a cracker, and topped it generously with smoked salmon. Then he reached over for a paper plate. As he did, his elbow jogged into someone. A plate of cheese and vegetables flew into the air and landed on the floor with a *splat!* Kyle looked up to see whose plate it was. Then he groaned inwardly. It was Dr Milikove's!

'Sir, I'm so sorry!' he blurted.

'Don't worry about it,' Dr Milikove replied jovially. 'This floor's seen worse. Hey, Nancy, bring a broom over here.'

Nancy bustled over with a broom and a dustpan. Dr Milikove took them from her and started sweeping.

'That's okay, I'll do it,' Kyle squeaked.

'I've got it.' Dr Milikove winked at him. 'I owe you one.'

Dr Milikove finished cleaning up and handed the broom back to Nancy. Kyle couldn't believe it. Could Dr Milikove actually be apologizing for yelling at him when he spilled water on his lab coat last week? Kyle grinned.

'I hope your lab coat's recovered, sir,' he said bravely.

Dr Milikove chuckled. 'Well, it was just water,' he said. Then he waved at Kyle and disappeared into the crowd.

'It's amazing what holidays do to people,' Kyle muttered aloud.

Nancy laughed. 'Yes, he seems almost human tonight, doesn't he? But don't worry – come next shift, he'll be the same old nasty, grumpy Dr Milikove we all love.'

'You think so?' Kyle said.

'Honey, I know it.' Nancy rolled her eyes and went back to the table to get more food. Kyle went with her and piled his plate high. He stood munching as the party got livelier. Someone had brought in a portable CD player and music was blaring through the room: a tape of Christmas favorites. Kyle's eyebrows rose when he recognized what was playing. It was Bing Crosby singing 'White Christmas.' Kyle's father used to always make them listen to that song every year on Christmas Eve. Personally, Kyle thought it was one of the corniest songs in the world, but at that moment, it felt just right.

Not to Dagger, though. Kyle turned to see Dagger standing beside him, a look of disgust on his face. 'Man, this song is lame,' Dagger said, shaking his head. 'Can't they find some Christmas music that wasn't written in prehistoric times?'

'Oh, Dagger, don't be such a grouch.' Max laughed.

'But this music hurts my ears!'

'My dad thinks it's the greatest,' Kyle confessed.

He laughed when Dagger said, 'That figures, man.'

The three of them stood there a minute in companionable silence. It was fun to see all the ER staff cutting loose for a change. Kyle's eyes popped as Dr Cohen invited Connie to waltz around the room with him.

'You know,' he said aloud, 'I wasn't looking forward to Christmas at all this year. But now I am.'

'How's your brother?' Max asked, a bit hesitantly.

'He's doing better,' Kyle replied. 'I just hope he can make it home for Christmas.'

'When will you know?' Dagger asked.

'Next week.'

'Well, man, I'll keep my fingers crossed for you.'

Kyle looked at Dagger in surprise. 'Thanks,' he said.

'So will I,' Max piped up. 'It's only fair. I already got my Christmas wish.'

'What, me?' Dagger grinned.

'No way!' Then Max blushed. 'I mean, sure. But that wasn't what I was thinking about. I was thinking about Ricardito. I was so scared he wouldn't have a real home after Teresa died. But I went and saw him yesterday, and everything is working out great with Hector and his wife.'

'You think Hector's wife is really comfortable with adopting Ricardito?' Dagger sounded unconvinced.

'Yeah.' Max nodded. 'I guess she really did have a change of heart when she saw Teresa dying. I was over there for a couple of hours and Carmen – that's Hector's wife – was great to Ricardito. He looked happy.'

'That's good to hear,' said Kyle. He looked around for Sara. She should be here with them. Then he saw her across the room talking to Ms Dominguez. Kyle scowled slightly.

Everything else was going better, but he still hadn't talked to Ms Dominguez about writing him his college recommendation after that extra shift he pulled. But he hadn't dared to ask. He didn't know what he would do if she said no.

Just then Ms Dominguez touched Sara on the arm and started walking across the room. It took Kyle a moment to realize she was coming toward him.

'Hi, Ms Dominguez.'

'Hello, Mr Cullen. Are you having fun?'

Kyle swallowed a big gulp of fruit punch. 'Yeah. Sure. It's a terrific party.'

Ms Dominguez smiled. 'It sure is.' Her eyes locked on Kyle's. 'I just wanted to let you know that I will be writing you a recommendation, Mr Cullen. I spoke to Martha Rodgers earlier tonight. She said you did a great job last week under very difficult circumstances.'

Kyle was silent for a moment. It was strange, but now that he had what he wanted, he didn't know how to react. 'Thank you,' he said at last. 'That's very nice of you. I know I've caused some trouble, and, well, I appreciate it.'

'That's all right,' Ms Dominguez replied stiffly. Then the corners of her mouth turned up just a little. 'Believe it or not, I do think you'll be a good doctor one day, Mr Cullen. Provided you remember one simple thing—'

'What's that?' Kyle inquired.

'Always obey the rules!'

'Don't worry. I will,' Kyle promised. Ms Dominguez nodded, then turned and moved through the crowd toward the refreshments.

'See?' a voice whispered at his elbow. 'She's not so bad.' It was Sara. Kyle looked down at her. Sara's eyes were shining. She looked happy.

Maybe she heard that Josh is coming back here for

the holidays or something, Kyle thought gloomily. 'So you hear from Josh lately?' he said aloud. As soon as the words were out of his mouth, he felt like kicking himself.

'Yeah. He's spending Hanukkah with his grandparents in Connecticut.'

'Oh,' said Kyle. His heart lifted. So Josh wasn't the reason Sara was in a such a good mood. Kyle couldn't believe that simple fact could make him feel so great.

Shortly he noticed the party was breaking up. He peered up at the clock on the wall and saw why. It was already after two in the morning!

'It's getting late,' Max said.

'Yeah,' Sara agreed. 'I should get going.' She looked at Kyle, and then at Max and Dagger. 'Are you guys all ready to go?'

'Yeah.' Max moved closer to Dagger and grinned. 'We're ready to go. But to tell the truth, we were thinking of going out for a burger. I know it's crazy after all this food here – but anyway, you guys want to come?'

Kyle was about to consider it, but Sara poked him in the back. 'Uh, no thanks,' he replied, glancing over at Sara, who was giving him the evil eye. 'I have to be up early.'

'So do I,' Sara said firmly.

'Oh well. See you guys next week,' Max said hurriedly. 'I'll call you tomorrow, Sara!'

'Okay. Later!' Sara said, as she and Kyle watched the two of them leave.

'What was that all about?' Kyle asked.

'Well, couldn't you see for yourself?'

Kyle chuckled. 'Yeah, only you didn't have to drill a hole into my back. I got the message.' Kyle looked at Sara. It had been a rough night, but she looked fresh and wide awake and strangely calm. He, on the other hand, still felt wired – so wired that he didn't feel like going home right away. 'So, do you want to go out for coffee or something?'

Sara didn't reply right away.

'I don't mean like a date,' he added hastily, thinking that maybe she thought he was trying to pick up on her. Well, wasn't he? 'Look,' he finally managed to say, 'I know you're still hung up on Josh. I'm not trying to be your boyfriend or anything. I just, you know, thought it might be nice to hang out and talk a little away from this place . . .' He was shocked at what he just said – and from the look on her face, so was Sara. Damn! Had he blown it? He did, after all, think Sara was a great girl. By saying he didn't want to be her boyfriend, had he just insulted her?

But Sara's look of surprise changed to one of

pleasure as she smiled. 'Thanks, Kyle. I'd love to go hang out with you for a little while,' she replied.

Kyle could not believe his good fortune.

'But let's go somewhere nearer to home, if you don't mind. I'm kind of creeped out by this area tonight after that bus accident and all those dead bodies.'

'It is pretty creepy,' he admitted. 'Can you believe it? I've never seen anything like that accident. I guess they were lucky it happened right in front of the hospital.'

Sara stopped at the rest room for a moment. While Kyle waited for her, he thought about the fact that he was actually going out with a girl for the first time since Alicia.

But Sara, she was something else. She wasn't just cute, she was smart and funny and really caring. He wondered if she would ever be able to think about him in that way, especially after Josh. That whole relationship had been pretty serious, and even though the guy was gone, Kyle could tell that she was still kind of into Josh. He and Sara had become friends after all this time volunteering, but she had never really reacted to his charm like other girls had. Weirdly, that made him like her even more.

Sara came out of the women's bathroom a few minutes later. 'How about Johnny Rocket's?' she said

'They have great veggie burgers and they're open all night. A lot of my friends go there after the movies and stuff. You could meet them.'

'Great! Some of my friends go there, too.' Although Sara was not his usual type of flamboyant girl, she was definitely someone he could be proud of being seen with *and* have a good time with. The idea made him feel nice. Unlike the usual apprehension he felt the first time out with a new girl, he was looking forward to spending as much time with Sara as possible – even if it was just as friends.

As they waited for an escort to take them out to the parking lot, they paused at the front entrance of the hospital and stared out at the lights of the hills behind CMH. The wind had picked up and had blown the smog out of the downtown area, leaving a view all the way to the top of Lookout Peak. Bright lights sparkled on the mountainside and made Kyle feel like he was somewhere far from the Emergency Room, far from the city.

He turned to look at Sara, her hair blowing around her face, her eyes bright as she looked into the distance. She shivered and pulled her jacket closer to her body, a little smile flitting across her face. He casually slid his arm around her and lightly squeezed, as if to tell her that he'd keep her warm. She stared out at the mountains with a peaceful look on her face. Kyle felt like he was on top of the world.